AUG 3 2016

ALLEGHENY FRONT

MATTHEW NEILL NULL

THE MARY MCCARTHY PRIZE IN SHORT FICTION
SELECTED BY LYDIA MILLET

SARABANDE BOOKS LOUISVILLE, KY

Library of Congress Cataloging-in-Publication Data

Null, Matthew Neill, 1984-
[Short stories. Selections]
Allegheny front : stories / by Matthew Neil null.—First edition.
pages ; cm
ISBN 978-1-941411-25-4 (pbk. : alk. paper)—ISBN 978-1-941411-26-1 (ebook)
I. Title.
PS3614.U8644A6 2016
813'.6--dc23
                        2015023360

Cover design and interior by Kristen Radtke.

Manufactured in Canada.
This book is printed on acid-free paper.

Sarabande Books is a nonprofit literary organization.

This project is supported in part by an award from the National Endowment for the Arts. The Kentucky Arts Council, the state arts agency, supports Sarabande Books with state tax dollars and federal funding from the National Endowment for the Arts.

for the animals

All this repeated cant, therefore, about our American mountains is not true in point of fact. But what if it were?—yes, gentlemen, what if it were? And this question brings me to the gist of the matter.

—Philip Pendleton Kennedy, *The Blackwater Chronicle: A Narrative of an Expedition into the Land of Canaan, of Randolph County, Virginia, a Country Flowing with Wild Animals, Such as Panthers, Bears, Wolves, Elk, Deer, Otter, Badger, &c., &c., with Innumerable Trout—by Five Adventurous Gentlemen, without Any Aid of Government, and Solely by Their Own Resources, in the Summer of 1851.*

ALLEGHENY FRONT

TABLE OF CONTENTS

Introduction by Lydia Millet

INTRODUCTION

ALLEGHENY FRONT HAS FEW SENTIMENTAL TRAPPINGS. Traveling salesmen meet up with the guns of the landed poor; tourists die, loggers die, cranky uncles are pulverized. But as often as men kill each other in Matthew Neill Null's singular, strong collection, they kill animals more. And not just game animals, either: black bears are massacred, bald eagles killed and crucified. In these intelligent and unpretentious stories, men's stubbornness is a rock face, their anger a crown fire, their occasional tenderness a rill.

In an era where even the more esoteric of literary fictions tend to have moved away from the rural, away from the beasts of the forests and fields, away from land-based individual sustenance and the rhythms of seasons and tide, Null's stories are remarkable for both their sharp relevance and their otherness. They seem to uncover a texture of living that's increasingly alien to urban readers, who, for better or worse, make up the lion's share of buyers and borrowers of contemporary literary fiction in the United States. It's a gritty texture precisely defined by the details of natural places, without the slickness and bright primary colors of highly engineered, exclusively human habitats. Null's subtler palette is browns and greens, yellows and grays, the blues of sky and water.

It'd be disingenuous of me to call these stories "authentic," since I'm frankly unqualified to judge the authenticity of foreign cultural representations—and make no mistake, the divide between rural and urban life in this country in 2016 is stark enough to make one foreign to the other. Of course, it's not a literal divide and is far more nuanced than this reductive formulation (for instance, I live in the middle of the desert in a warm, red state, but I grew up urban and cold, and I don't change my own flats).

Still, we who live it know it instinctively: there are at least two nations at odds with each other here and now, a profound schism dividing their dominant cultures. (Journalist Colin Woodard has famously, and with fairly minimal controversy, put the number of geocultural nations within our formal national boundaries higher, in fact, at eleven—and in Woodard's scheme Null's literary homeland of West Virginia is itself split into three cultures, two rural-based and only one small northern part "Yankee.")

So, like much of my reading demographic, I know almost as little of hardscrabble country life in West Virginia as it's possible to know. But I know a bit about land-use policy, a smidgeon about wildlife management, and a fair amount about natural resource conflicts, and Null's stories have an extensive grounding in all of these. They interest themselves in the brutality with which we've plundered our legacy of wild places, in the excruciating social limits that drive personal choices, and the economic corners into which we paint each other and ourselves. Almost every piece touches on some part of the class enmity that festers between rich and poor, educated and uneducated, those who understand the land as a treasure to be protected and those who eke out a tough living directly from it.

Yet *Allegheny Front* is anything but one-sided or simplistically dualistic. It remains at a distance from judgment, at a remove from easy definitions, unspooling a lucid and often painful history of appetite, exploitation, and bereavement.

—Lydia Millet

SOMETHING YOU CAN'T LIVE WITHOUT

THREADGILL HAD BEEN ONE OF THEM, or something like it. This part of the world hadn't been penetrated by the Company in four seasons, ever since they lost him, their ace drummer, on the Blackwater River, where he'd been shot off a farmer's wife by the farmer himself. While the man fumbled a fresh shell into the breech of his shotgun, Threadgill ran flopping out the back door and tumbled down the sheer cliff behind the cabin. There he came to rest in the arms of a mighty spruce. The tree held him like a babe till they rigged up a block and tackle to lift him out. They said he had nothing but socks on, argyle. The image bored into Cartwright's brain like a weevil. The week the Company hired Cartwright on as a drummer, he found the dead man's sucker list wrapped in oilskin and tacked under the wagon tongue. It was the secret of Cartwright's success. He grew flush off commission in no time.

Polishing a new gold tooth with his tongue, Cartwright clattered down the road in a buckboard wagon. He followed the split-rail fence that wormed along the trace. Ironweed and seven sisters grew between the ruts, tickling the horses—a gelded pair of blood bays. The farther he traveled, the more the roadbed degraded. The spring rains had gnawed small ravines into it all the way down to the shining black chert; he kept his horses to a low canter, should they come upon a slip. The tunnel of rain-lush forest gave way, finally, to cleared farmland around the bend.

The only thing Cartwright knew about McBride, today's prospect, was that the farmer was a sucker, though the few neighbors around there would have told Cartwright that no one knew the valley better than honest Sherman McBride—the creeks that bred trout, the caves that held flint—except for the two boys he raised off those mouthfuls of corn that rose from the fields and strained for sun. Even so, honesty would be the man's downfall. Cartwright gazed up at the Allegheny Mountains that were a series of blue lines on the horizon. This was long before the forests were scoured off the mountains and the coal chipped from their bellies, before blight withered the chestnut stands. A dozen passenger pigeons trickled through the sky, the first Cartwright had seen that year despite all his travels. The cherry of his cigarette tumbled, and he jumped and slapped it out of his lap.

Ah! The passenger pigeons he remembered best of all. Every fall, his family had waited for the black shrieking cloud. Word was passed down from northern towns—Anthem, Mouth of Seneca—and there they were, a pitch river of millions undulating in the sky. When they touched down to rest, they toppled the crowns from oaks. They plucked any living plant and then the roiling swarm fell to the ground and tore at grass. Under them, no one could tell field from road.

"Whoever cut this grade," Cartwright said to the horses, "must have followed a snake up the hollow. Followed a damned snake!" He roomed near the courthouse in Anthem, but he hadn't been there in seven weeks. He was deep into the summer swing through the highland counties, all the way up to Job and Corinth, the old towns once called Salt Creek and Beartown

MATTHEW NEILL NULL

until a religious fervor inspired their rechristening. Cartwright glanced at the crate jostling under the tarp. He said, "Damn, boys. I'd almost buy it myself to get shut of this situation."

He swabbed his face with his tie. Soon, the sun burned off the fog and hoisted itself into the sky. "Horses, it's hotter than two rats fucking in a wool sock. I tell you that much."

He took another little drink. Bottle-flies turned their emerald backs in the sun. Young monarchs gathered to tongue the green horseshit and clap their wings.

Before the Company hired him, Cartwright had sold funeral insurance, apprenticed himself to a farrier, and, in his youth, worked his father's acres. To hear his father tell it, Anthem was a profane place, and the family would do well to keep ground between their children and such ways. But a month after she buried her husband, Cartwright's mother closed the deed on their land and moved them to Anthem without debate. Her sister lived by the railroad depot.

Though it had been years since he'd swung a scythe or sheathed his arms in the hot blood of stock, Cartwright's boyhood helped him build a quick rapport, or so he said, with the farmers who bought his wares. Truthfully, he bullied them into buying the tools, or, if they would not be bullied, he casually insulted the farmers' methods in front of their wives. "That's one way of doing things," he said to the hard sells. "Gets it done sure as any other. Yessir. Hard labor! Of course, you don't see many men doing it that way anymore. Last season, I found blue-gums down in Greenbrier County working like that."

"You don't say."

"No, excuse me. Season before last. And they might have been Melungeons. Ma'am, could you spare some water for a wayfaring traveler?"

Cartwright would bid them good night and retreat to the hayloft, and, as often as not, be greeted in the morning by the farmer with a fistful of wrinkled dollars and watery, red-rimmed eyes, having been flayed the night long for stubborn habits that clashed with the progressive spirit of the times.

Like his own father, the people Cartwright sold to worked rocky mountain acres, wresting little more than subsistence from the ground. None had owned slaves. Some abstained from the practice out of moral doctrine; most abstained for lack of money. They carded their own wool, cured their own tobacco, and died young or back-bent, withered and brown as ginseng roots twisted from the soil. A handful of affluent farmers in the river bottoms owned early Ford tractors, odd and exoskeletal; the rest still worked mules and single-footed plows. Cartwright had seen acres of corn on hillsides canting more than forty-five degrees.

To even the humblest farmers, still he managed to sell a few harrow teeth or ax-heads.

Success ensnared him: the more he found, the more desolate the places the Company sent him to, and the higher the profits they came to expect. He was the rare man to wring dollars from these scanty places, and he'd grown tired of the counties they cast him farther and farther into like a bass plug. A man couldn't even buy a fresh newspaper where he roamed. Cartwright brought these people the first word of laws and statutes that a young state government was trying to filigree over the backcountry. He should have said no, but the Company representative appealed to his vanity: "I'll be straight with you. We're in the middle of a recession and"—the man was a veteran of the Spanish War—"we need our best on the ramparts. We know you can make quota, buddy. You done proved yourself." The praise flooded Cartwright's belly with a singing warmth, sure as a shot of clean bourbon. Only now did he realize the Company had taken advantage of his loyalty. As soon as he hit Anthem, he'd demand a promotion.

Cartwright took the last hit of whiskey and licked his lips.

"My ass hurts," he told the horses through a sly, sidelong grin. "Do your feet hurt? Huh now?"

Now there was the trouble of the last plow; never had he returned with inventory, and he wasn't about to start. Had to make quota. Cartwright lobbed the jar into a roadside holly bush, where it left a quivering hole in the leaves. "Hup," he said, slapping the horses' haunches with the reins. The sweat went flying. A swarm of insects gathered to sup at the horses' soft eyes, nostrils, assholes. He began to doze, but a furry gray deerfly tagged him on the neck. He slapped it away and cursed softly, so not to spook the horses. Blood formed, round and perfect as a one-carat ruby. Again, he lifted his tie.

McBride seemed to be getting up a small orchard of thorny apples along the road. The split rails of the fence became fresher till they gave out—around the bend, Cartwright found two boys planing and setting lengths of locust by the roadside. Fresh from the adze, the cut lumber gleamed silver in the sun, if marred in places by heartshakes and spalting. The boys wore a coarse homespun, bearing the scurvy look of those who live without women. Their long hair was cut severely, as if it had been chopped with a mattock.

Over the *chip-chop-thunk* of the adze, the twins spoke to each other in a fluttering brogue, the voice of orioles. They saw the wagon and fell dumb, tools gone limp in their hands. They openly stared. Cartwright reined his horses and said, "Hello there, fellows. You the men of the place?"

While one answered, the other spat on the blade of the scrub plane and ran it grating over a stone. The boy said, "English barn a quarter mile up. Ought to find him there. You a preacher?"

"No."

"Ah. That's too bad. We haven't heard good preaching in a while." Cartwright wouldn't have guessed it, but both of the boys could cipher well. The eldest had read the family Bible seven times through. The one on the left asked, "You play music?"

"No."

"Not the taxman, are you?"

"I'm a salesman."

The boy had no comment for this. Waving Cartwright on, he opened a mouthful of teeth so black and broken they looked serrated. He stuffed tobacco inside. Cartwright thanked both boys and slapped his horses forward. The wagon went rattling on.

When the drummer was out of earshot, one asked, "What do you think?"

"I expect he'll expect us to feed him dinner."

His brother sighted down the scrub plane, eyeing it for flaws. "Need that like a hot nail in the foot."

"Least he's not here for taxes."

"At least."

The twins turned away, shouldered a rail in tandem, set it atop another.

Catholic Irish, Cartwright thought, like his mother's father, who'd been converted to the Southern Methodist Church when the preacher said how the Pope's Catholics was little better than cannibals, eating up the body of Christ and carving the thumbs off of saints. The body is profane, the spirit real! As a boy, he had heard a Catholic in an infirmary pray to beads. They had come here to dig railroad tunnels, but, like exotic flowers, never quite took to the place and died about as quickly as the land would have them.

Soon he came upon a sharp-shouldered man plowing up earth with acres to go. The farmer's face was sallow and long-whiskered under a broad-brimmed felt hat, but his hands and arms were the color of leaf tobacco. His boots had been mended with baling twine. McBride, for sure. He whoa'd the mule to a stop. The animal was stout and gleamed wetly in the sun, like a doused ingot of iron. Waves of salt had dried on its shoulders.

"Hi," the drummer said, lifting a hand from the reins. "Good-looking animal you got there."

"Ought to be," McBride said. He took off his crushed felt hat and swept it across his forehead like a bandanna. "We paid big on him at the auction. My last mule lived to be thirty-two years old. Hell, my neighbor just give him to me on trade and we worked him swaybacked. After the war, it was. Know how much the price on a mule goes up in thirty-two years?"

Cartwright wanted to say, It's called capital, old buddy. Instead, he politely inquired as to what the years could do to the price of a mule.

"Enough to take a belt of the good stuff before raising my bidding hand."

Cartwright shook his head knowingly. "It's an animal you can't do without."

"Indeed. Like I tell my boys, you can't do without a mule no more than you can do without legs. You're a cripple without one. Don't I, boys? Don't I say you can't do without a mule no more than legs?"

"Yes. He says it all the damn time." The boys had stalked up from behind. Cartwright couldn't help but jump.

"I told you," McBride said. "All the damn time I say it."

Cartwright regained his composure. The pitch: "You speak with a lot of sense and experience. Fellows, a mule is important and so's a man's tools. I was a farmer for many years and indeed I know that a farmer is only good as his tools. Let the harness match the hide, as they say. You need something to equal that good mule."

McBride flinched. A less experienced drummer might think this the wrong tack, but Cartwright knew his trade, and his trade was talk. In his mind's eye he saw the contents of the Irishman's barn: cracked and broken harnesses, homemade harrows, antiquated briar hoes—all tools of the Old World. They might even shell corn by hand. "Yessir," he continued, "I got something here that will double, if not triple, a man's yield at harvest with only half the effort. Half the effort, twice the yield. Powerful math. Now how about that?"

McBride said nothing. The good mule stood in the furrow, radiating a potent silence. The best draft animals have no discernible personality, and this one seemed such a beast.

"Now me," Cartwright said, "I'd say you couldn't beat that with a stick. This tool a man can't afford to be without. Latest from Virginia Progressive Agriculture. Help me, boys."

The twins pitched forward. Cartwright dismounted, whispered into the horses' toggling ears, and walked around to the wagon-bed. He peeled back a yellow oilskin, revealing a rectangular crate. He took out a small pry bar and removed a series of staples. The twins helped him lift the lid off a steel-pointed, double-footed plow packed in straw. It had been polished to a violent gleam, and the sun caught and danced like hooked minnows on every point and angle. McBride didn't dare look back, imagining his own single-footed plow: crude, hand-forged, nicked and dull as any kitchen blade.

"Brand new, our latest model. This here is the McCrory Reaper," Cartwright said, "but I call it the Miracle Plow. Our engineers have designed it to render a maximum harvest as far as crops go, clearing twice as much land in the same amount of hours and cutting a deeper furrow, turning up fresher soil and more nutrients. We guarantee better crops or your money back. It's been tested by a scientist at the state college for three years and the results have been proved.

"Look. I'm not the first drummer to come down the road and won't be the last, but I sell no snake oil. I'm a farm boy myself, grew up on a spread the size of this one. I know what it's like to rise with the last star and work under the light of the first. We lost that farm because we had two bad years running." Cartwright licked his mouth with the moisture of the lie. "That's all it took: two bad ones. I say with confidence, if we'd've had the McCrory Reaper, we'd still be farming my dad's acres. But my dad wasn't progressive. Wouldn't change with the times. Now another's working our land—successfully, with the Miracle Plow. Sold it to him myself. Broke my heart, too. Probably shouldn't be telling it, but I did. You got to get that dollar. Boys, help me move this thing. If you don't mind, Mr. McBride, let's unbuckle your old plow and hitch up this one. You got a singletree? No? That's okay. Let's run a couple furrows with it, free of charge, and see how it measures up. Break a half-acre. Would you be averse?"

The question hung there. The twins looked to McBride for instruction, eyes black and hard. Cartwright saw one boy had only nine fingers—a way to tell them apart. McBride gave them a slight nod. They harnessed the Miracle Plow.

Tucking his tie between the buttons of his shirt, Cartwright approached the mule as the Irishmen sat on their haunches in an outbuilding's shade. It was awkward for them to watch another man work without falling in line behind him. They rebelled against their jittering tendons, forced themselves still.

Cupping the mule's nose, Cartwright said, "You got to get to know a mule, right? What's his name? Ronald? Is that right? Ronald, do I have a treat for you. This thing's going to feel light as a vest." He moved behind the double-footed plow, leaned forward, and slapped the mule on its ass with a sharp tack fitted on the inside of his ring. The mule surged forward, the leather harness yanked with such force it began to groan.

"Jesus," McBride whispered. "Look at Ronald pull."

"This way, you're working the ground, and *it* ain't working you," Cartwright said, chewing on the poor food. "I hate to say it, but it's true. These days a man can't hope to compete without one."

They took supper in the kitchen, the core of a three-room dog-trot, dredging up beans and their white, watery gruel with a great circle of cornbread that McBride had cooked in a deep skillet, scooping the golden meal from a sack that stood open beside the woodstove. The meal had quite a grit to it, so the cornbread of-fered no flavor and the consistency of damp sawdust. Cartwright choked it down, thinking, Promotion, promotion. The sullen boys ate little, seeming to draw their fire from tobacco and wee hits of whiskey from a jug, which they didn't attempt to conceal, nor did they offer to share.

Cartwright and McBride discussed the merits and dimen-sions of the new plow at length. Look how effortlessly it turned the earth. Like a knife through hot bread, McBride kept saying, shaking his head. It barely wears on the mule, barely at all.

Cartwright looked about the room. Why'd Threadgill even note these people? Yet the sucker list read SHERMAN MCBRIDE in lovely, arching script. It made no sense. Even if McBride sold everything in this cabin and hid every cent from the government, he still couldn't scrape together fifteen dollars, not even with a straight razor pressed to his turkeyneck. These people were prime candidates for Moses's jubilee. Perhaps there was a relation who could lend them the money, with interest.

Come nightfall, McBride scratched up some fodder for Cart-wright's horses and showed him to the barn loft. McBride bid him good night and retreated to the cabin. A shining sliver of moon rested on the planks, and blue foxfire wafted on the hills. Shiver-ing in the cool of the evening, Cartwright stood in the barn door and watched Orion wheel in his chase.

Then he saw the twins standing in the twilight. They draped ancient flintlocks over their shoulders, the heavy octagonal bar-rels tamped with cut-nails and brass buttons. Not far away, a boar hog threw itself against the stall and bawled out, raking tusks against the wood. If a man fell in, it would leave nothing but a skull plate. Cartwright looked at the guns.

"They got a fox pinned on the mountain," the ten-fingered boy said. "Sometimes they cross the river here at the cut. Might get us a shot. Hear them hounds a-singing?"

Bound in a nimbus of light, the boys cocked their ears as if to a phonograph for music.

"There a bounty on it?" Cartwright asked.

Oh yeah, the boys said. They named a good figure. Maybe a piece of that plow, they hinted. They said it carefully, their green young minds grappling with the hard currency of commerce. "I see you looking at my hand," the maimed boy said, holding it up to the lantern.

Cartwright's stomach coiled.

"Lost it baiting a jaw-trap. Hand slipped." He looked Cartwright in the eye and said it bluntly, without threat; he hadn't lived in a civilized town yet. He hadn't learned shame.

"We put too much oil to it," the other said. "Got it slickery."

"Easy mistake to make," Cartwright said, relieved. "Do you cure them or bounty them?"

"Depends if the fur traders or the government men are coming around," the ten-fingered boy said. "Neighbors send word up the road."

"You know," Cartwright said, "an animal has just enough brains to cure its own hide, be it deer, fox, or bear. Something to study on, I'd say."

The boys thought on it for a minute. "That is something," the nine-fingered boy said. "I never thought of it. Wouldn't call it a puzzle, but it's something to note."

A grin tugging at the corners of his mouth, the ten-fingered boy said, "You *was* a farmer."

"Oh yeah," Cartwright said, smiling. "Them was good times."

"Huh. We'll have to talk some more about that plow."

Before they left, they slipped him a twist of tobacco, as they would to a neighbor. Cartwright snapped his fingers, twice. He was in with them now.

Cartwright climbed the rungs of the ladder to his nest. The drummer was careful with his cigarette, cleaning the boards with his shoe and killing the cinder on the wood. Then he heard a woman screaming on the mountain, but remembered it was merely the cry of a gray fox, a dog that walks trees like a cat. He leaned back, breathing the ancient smell of cured apples and tobacco hanging from the rafters. Also, a whiff of swallow droppings.

The smell brought to mind his father, mother, brothers, sisters. Cartwright's family took up pine-stobs, brooms, and pokers, beating pigeons to death by the dozens. His father lined them up on the ground, and his sister Audrey broke kindling to fire the kettle and scald the feathers from the bodies. They gorged themselves, like every other hard-up family from Canada to Texas. The birds were nothing less than manna, and their soil fell like flakes of lime, his mother and sisters holding umbrellas straining over their heads to keep it off their dresses. What they couldn't eat, they ground into fertilizer. Back and forth, his sisters carried the pailfuls of feathers and pulp. The flocks blotted the sun and spooked the horses, which tried to crop grass to the verge of foundering because they weren't ready, at midday, to return slack-bellied to the barn and stand hungry in the darkness. The screaming clouds peeled back the green table of grass, and the horses chewed faster, faster.

Cartwright's brother Nige handed him a dead passenger pigeon to play with. He turned it over in his hands: the red eye set there like a hardened drop of blood, the slaty guard feathers the color of water churning over the bottoms of rivers that hold trout. The body was limp in his hand, neck lolling about as he stroked the saffron underbelly. In his trunk in Anthem, he now kept that mummified pair of wings, feathers still crisp as fletching against his thumb. Wrapped in black gauze and smelling sweetly of dry mold, they could have been torn from its back just yesterday. He would wrap them back up and put them away under his winter clothes. There were damn few pigeons left now and someday the sky would be evacuated of everything but rain, airships, and stars.

MATTHEW NEILL NULL

Cartwright turned and felt a sharp corner dig into his kidney. He plunged his arm into the straw and came up with a jar of corn. "Hallelujah," he said, grinning. He held the clear liquor up to a moon as hollow and weird as Thomas Jefferson's death mask. He turned the jar, and the moon's geography warped and spilled to the corners. With luck like this, he'd be back in Anthem in no time. He unscrewed the two-piece lid with a grainy, skirling sound.

After taking a third of the jar, Cartwright made a nest in the straw and settled into a dream-sleep rife with women. He was a man of low station, a virgin at twenty-five. He wouldn't be Thread-gill, though. Cartwright wanted a steady woman. Regional Manager pay would get him one. Maybe she'd have earth to till, a few acres. Yes, she would. He cocked his ear. The gray fox screamed.

The nine-fingered boy said, "Here it comes, dollar bills on the foot," and his brother laughed a laugh as dry as cornhusks. The boys waited for the fox under a wash of stars. There were hunts, too, writ in the sky above: the hare, the dogs greater and lesser, and the Great Hunter whipping them on.

A square of sun teased Cartwright's face and chest in the morning. Blinking, he glanced about the loft, trying to remember where he was. Swallows peeked out of their mudnests and streaked blue and gold out the window. He woke to their piping, and McBride called him out of the barn. In the kitchen, a tray of sloppy eggs was laid out and a kettle whistled. The tea had the musty tang of roots, or the kettle had been used to make chicory coffee, one. Cartwright asked if the boys had shot themselves a fox. McBride said he supposed they had not.

"That's a shame," Cartwright said. "Bounty's a good way to turn a few dollars."

McBride flinched. Cartwright meant to spur a conversation of whether McBride wanted to buy or not—his back ached from sleeping strangely and a bouncing wagon might cure it—

but like these mountain people do, McBride shunned talk of money and led the drummer in an elliptical conversation that touched upon foxes, what foxes eat, foxes and chickens, bounties, plows, planting by the signs, the Stations of the Cross, the months of the moon, the death of his wife in the winter, TB, washing handkerchiefs of red roses, foxes again, plows again, and, finally, the matter of money. McBride counted out pennies, paper bills, and a lone Quarter Eagle, building them into a small pile.

Cartwright frowned, plucking off the Confederate note the man placed on top—a two-dollar Judah Benjamin—and setting it aside. He said, "This is only half, I'm afraid. Barely half." It was time to go. Experience told him that McBride was about to offer him goats and old boots to make up the difference.

"I know this," McBride said. "But you said it yourself, this is a tool a man can't do without. I got something to cover the rest. It's out where the flints are, just sitting in the ground. It can be sold back where you come from for great profit."

"If you're talking about ginseng or hides, I don't truck in that," Cartwright said, the tooth flickering as he spoke.

"The agent buys hides all the time."

"Look, you don't understand. *I* don't buy them. Too much bother. Town-people don't barter no more. The Company says I got to take federal money. Legal tender. I had a fellow wanted to give me a rarefied sidelock shotgun all the way from Italy and I couldn't take it."

"This goes beyond your typical deal. This is five shotguns. Cover the plow and more and you can have the rest for your troubles."

Cartwright looked about the room. No. If McBride had some silver buried about the place, it wouldn't be such a wreck. "Well," Cartwright said, standing up, not even bothering to hide his disgust, "I'll be taking my leave of you, Mr. McBride. Good luck with your yield. Got to find somebody who can actually buy this thing."

MATTHEW NEILL NULL

When Cartwright went out the door, it was the serene way that McBride said, "You'll regret it," that called him back. The Irishman took a folded piece of newspaper from his wallet and smoothed it out on the knife-scored table. "I had to go to Jephthah for court day. I was on the jury that hung that Brad fellow for jiggering his little niece and I got this off the corner-man."

Cartwright read it once, and read it again. McBride said, "I know where you can get one of them, a great big one."

"Why ain't you got it out already?"

"Thought you said you was a farmer," McBride said, bristling. "Anthem's more than sixty mile. You can't go leaving."

"Hey now, settle down," said Cartwright. "I ain't casting aspersions." He read the notice a third time, a grin swelling on his face. "We'll split it sixty-forty," he said. "But that's a *solid* forty."

No one had been to the cave much since the War, when a few dozen men harvested saltpeter for the Confederacy, and then for the Union when the militia told them they lived no longer in Old Virginia. They'd shrugged, saying, Makes no difference to us, we just want to eat. And avoid conscription, they might have added. When the War ended, their profits vanished and the cave was plunged back to obscurity. A scattering of people knew the place, but none knew it like McBride's boys: they crawled into the Sinks of Gandy to harvest flint and hide from downpours when they hunted spring turkeys.

Toting a bundle of tools, the nine-fingered boy led Cartwright on cattle paths to skirt their few neighbors, suspicious people loyal to no one but blood and that even questionable. They wandered into high meadows drowning in beaver dams and dropped into the next valley. A thin jade river fled north and drained with a sucking roar into the Sinks of Gandy, a hatchet-wound that grinned in the mountainside. The Sinks led to a lacework of caverns that under-girded the farmlands. The river resurfaced three miles north-by-northwest.

Stubby stalactites drooped from the opening, and a hush issued from the hole, exhaling the smell of damp rock. Cartwright held out a hand and found it too mild for hell. He glanced over his shoulder at the humpy valley-land beckoning him back. "Two miles in," the boy said, stuffing his belongings into a waterproof satchel made of stomach. "Long miles."

They were swallowed into the cold bowels of the mountain. Cartwright cursed, sinking his leg into a sump of cave mud as the boy lit a pineknot from his satchel. The torch spat glow on soapstone walls that glistened wetly as a dog's mouth.

A frothy roar. Crotch-deep in the river, their flesh shriveled. All manner of beasts erupted from the crevices—blind wormy salamanders, hare-eared bats whose wings were silk fans brushing their faces. They scrambled over rocks and hangs as the river dropped and narrowed, sluicing through a trough. Deeper they went. Walls closed and they squeezed through closets of stone, rooms within rooms. Cartwright felt his chest cave, his ribs compress. Each breath painful, space no more than a corncrib. His lungs burned. He cried out, casting echoes through the tunnel.

"Quit your wailing," the boy said, holding out his hand to the mud-smeared man who *still* wore a necktie. "Breathe deep. Scoot sideways."

Cartwright popped free into a chapel of stone. The boy pulled a fresh pineknot from his bag, touched it off, and handed the hissing lantern to the drummer. The room soared overhead, massive wet ribbons of rock dripping in folds from the ceiling. The chemical burn of waste in his nostrils, a roof of rodents screeching above. In bygone days the men said, The bats sow shit and we reap gunpowder.

They came to an opening, a single slur of light on the floor. Cartwright stuck his head inside and drank the sweet air. Covered crown to boot in coffee-colored mud, he asked, "Won't that fire choke us?"

The boy ran his four fingers over the remains of abandoned saltpeter hoppers pegged to the wall, troughs of cucumber wood and oak. "Big window up top lets the fire out. Indian smokehouse. Funny thing, you walk though the field and a flock of bats just pop out the ground beneath you. You near piss yourself."

They felt the earth settle and creak, the animals shuddering in waves overhead. A few squeaking kits fell from the ceiling, and they couldn't help but tromp them under boot.

"What if the whole mountain falls down?"

"Been standing since Genesis," the boy said. "Look, here we are."

The ground was a carpet of fossilized dung. With their torches, they studied the wall-scratchings of a lost people, charcoal men in positions of coupling and war. That's when Cartwright saw the face glaring back at him. The maw of a cave bear jutted from the rock, trapped by flood long ago. The greasy pine fire burned against it with a contained fury, illuminating the hollows of its face. It was no middling circus bear, its skull gargantuan, with black canines dripping down the jaw. Cartwright couldn't believe it. He put a hand to the wall, and soft shale flaked and fell away. He took the clipping from his shirt pocket and read it aloud, taking a second go at the longer words.

REPRESENTATIVE OF THE SMITHSONIAN INSTITUTE TO AP-PEAR AT ANTHEM CHAMBER OF COMMERCE—COMPENSATION FOR FOSSILS OF PREHISTORIC MEGAFAUNA. *One of the state's most famous visitors, Thomas Jefferson, found rare claw-bones of a giant three-toed sloth in the Organ Cave, on the old Nat Hinkle farm in Greenbrier County in 1792. Dr. Charles Lands Burke, a young scholar from Washington, D.C., seeks to follow in his footsteps and is looking to local landowners for aid with this gov-ernment initiative—with generous compensation.*

"Sounds right to me," the boy said. Could the boy even have read it? Did someone explain it to him? He took a hammer and a chisel from his bag and handed them to Cartwright. Turning his shoulder so the boy couldn't see, Cartwright folded the newspaper clipping back into the sucker list, marrying the two documents together, and tucked them into his jacket.

Stepping forward, Cartwright ran his thumb against the sharp ring of the occipital bone and the worn points of fang, tracing the fissures of the skull that rippled like stitches under his touch. It thrilled him. He couldn't wait to turn it over in his hands. He was amazed there were such things in the ground, waiting to be dug out like potatoes. Cupping them in his brown palm, Cartwright's father used to show off the arrowheads he tilled out of the fields.

The boy said, "Something, ain't it?"

A scene came drifting up from the lakebed of memory. When Cartwright was seven years old, his father had bought a gold locket for his wife's birthday from a drummer passing through. A smile they hadn't seen before took hold of her face. A week later, his father stood clutching the doorframe, looking shamefully at where the false gold stained her pale skin like gangrene. He tore it from her neck and threw it down the well. It was the one time his father had cried in front of them. The frightened children fanned into the woods. That night, Cartwright's father had to come looking for him with a lantern to fetch him back home.

Cartwright grooved the chisel's tooth into the base of the skull, where the spine would fuse, and lifted the hammer. He let it fall. The chisel jumped in his hand and half the skull turned to silt. It cascaded down the rock wall with the faintest sigh. The boy let out a string of oaths so profane, so unparalleled, that surely they'd been inspired by a hell so near.

Cartwright was glad to have a hammer in hand.

Once again they waded the river, water sucking at their limbs. A pinprick of light appeared ahead. Neither spoke, even when a toothy rock tore Cartwright's jacket with a startling rip. Soon, a delicate sun and then a javelin of light struck the drummer's chest. They came to the mouth of the Sinks of Gandy. "I see them coming," the boy said.

Indeed, McBride and the ten-fingered boy stood there with guns in hand, laughing, each with a fox draped over his shoulder. McBride held a double-barreled sixteen-gauge loaded with pumpkin-ball slugs, a gun the drummer hadn't seen before. They lifted their bloody foxes to the sun. They were fresh, tongues still pink with the suggestion of life. The foxes couldn't be eaten, only sold; like all predators, they reeked of the flesh they'd consumed. One was a black-socked vixen with a sleek coat, the other a gray fox, its face and limbs streaked with red, which had obviously been living in a briar patch. It could use a currycomb and wouldn't bring as much, Cartwright mused miserably, but still a good price.

"You all get it?" McBride asked. "Them bones don't look like much, but they say it's money in the bank."

"Ask your drummer here," the nine-fingered boy said, cocking his head.

"That skull was too old! No one told me how old it was. That was damaged goods."

McBride colored. "Good what now?"

"It's in a thousand pieces," the boy said. "You couldn't broom it out of the dirt."

Cartwright opened his hands. "That skull wasn't worth a damn. You misled me. You violated our contract."

"Misled you?"

"That's the law. It's contract."

"We shook hands," the farmer said, looking to his boys. "Drummer, you said a man can't do without it."

"It's the law. The legislature wrote it. We just got to live by it."

"What? What are we going to do about that plow?"

"Hey now," Cartwright said, "don't bounty them foxes. Tan the hides and sell them. You'll turn a better profit. You get a few more dozen and I'll come back in the fall."

"Know how long it'll take to cure these hides?"

Cartwright said nothing.

"That's right. You'll be off down the road and we won't see you for a year. Hell, two year. You'll come back when you feel like it. Where will we be? I'm tired of this ground working me, I'm ready to work *it*. You said it yourself."

The nine-fingered boy said, "What's this?"

The boy knelt and picked up a folded piece of paper. Cartwright felt the world turn on a pivot. He grew light-headed and loose-limbed, as if he'd just been bled with leeches. The boy peeled the sucker list away from the newspaper clipping. His eyes scanned the lines. Cartwright thought about running, but he didn't know the way back to the road.

The nine-fingered boy read the words aloud, which listed the name McBride among the county's daft, drunken, gullible, and insane.

"Says we got an eye for any piece of metal, long as it's shiny. Drills, reapers. Pine away for it, we will."

"No better than crows," his brother said.

Cartwright opened his mouth, then let it shut with a click. He felt weary from the cave, and the years on the road, and his entire body was slick with mud, pant legs heavy as dragnets. He leaned against a sycamore that lorded over the Sinks of Gandy. He could retch.

"Look," he cried, "I know what it's like! I'm from here!"

With a crack, the nine-fingered boy slapped a creeping

armored caterpillar off his pant leg. "Jesus Christ," he said, looking down. It was a brilliant green, nearly five inches long. He looked back to Cartwright.

The slug punched Cartwright's side like a party ballot. The drummer fell against the slippery bark, and the shot patch fluttered against his face, a sulfur burn in his nostrils. Once, when he was young, he'd tasted a bitter pinch of gunpowder and said it tasted like a chimney. His father laughed, clamping a loving paw on the boy's shoulder, his palm rough as a file. Cartwright threw up a hand and the second shot took his forearm in a hail of bone and the third struck his chin, unhinging the mouth.

When Cartwright fell, he did it watching the light play through clouds on the face of the mountain.

McBride laid the shotgun on the ground and reached for a pipe of tobacco, hand shaking.

The ten-fingered boy asked, "What was that on your leg?"

"Hell if I know."

The boys turned the dragon-like caterpillar on a stick, its orange spikes waving. They ran their thumbs across them. The spikes were hard as apple-thorns.

"That's called a Hickory Devil," McBride said, turning back to the drummer's body. "Digs into the ground and turns into a big old red moth."

"Kill it," one said. "It'll kill a dog if it eats it."

Tartly, McBride said, "Don't. That's a myth. It won't hurt nothing."

It was a lonely place, and they merely covered the drummer in pine boughs, confident that no one would find him and no one would care. They should have known better, for the bears and the foxes broke him apart and scattered him far and near. Rodents gnawed his belt and boot leather for their share of salt. Five years later, a hunter found Cartwright's brass belt-buckle in the leaves and slipped it into his pocket.

It says something of the quality of the buckle's manufacture, as well as the hunter's eye, for it was the fourth week of October and the leaves were a thousand shades of brown, mottled like the skin on a copperhead's back. Later, some lost boys from Moatstown found part of him but paid it little mind, thinking him a deer because they failed to check the long, lithe bones for hooves or fingers. In twenty years, a bear hunter pried the gold tooth from his jaw and threw the husk to the ground. An old woman of Palatine German stock gave his ribcage a Christian burial after a dog dragged it behind her springhouse. She chanted the verses, murmuring, "Thorns and thistles shall it bring forth to thee, and thou shalt eat the herb of the field. In the sweat of thy face shalt thou eat bread, till thou return unto the ground. For dust thou art, and unto dust shalt thou return." But she was fading herself, near death, and troubled in her mind. Is only his torso in heaven? she wondered. Do his legs dance in hell? She was too frail to go searching for the rest, though his pelvic bone rested near a prominent fork in the road, gathering dry leaves like a crock.

The three Irishmen painted Cartwright's wagon black and set the smart new plow behind the mule in its traces. With a searing poker, they smeared the blood bays with their own brand. Cartwright would have recognized the sound of crackling flesh, because it sounded like the red-hot horseshoes he dropped hissing into a water barrel in his days as a farrier's apprentice.

After the day's excitement, McBride and his boys eased back into the rhythms of planting and sowed their corn. They enjoyed a typical harvest, green spears coming up straight and tasseled in mean if nourishing numbers. They chewed the lining of their cheeks in wonder, but then again, they'd merely completed their task with the Miracle Plow, a quarter of the fields. Next year would be the true test. The earth turned and cooled, and they waited out the long winter like denned bears, wagering on next year's harvest.

MATTHEW NEILL NULL

When next harvest came, they would have killed Cartwright all over again. The Miracle Plow had failed to increase their yield by any measure whatsoever, no better than the one it had replaced. When Cartwright's replacement came down the road three years later, they told him so. He urged on his horses with a grim flick of the traces.

As for the three Irishmen, they never roamed beyond the Sinks of Gandy, they waited each year for the trickle of passenger pigeons, they reposed in the ground with the cave bears. Leaning against the completed fence, each lit a clay pipe, savoring the ache of a day's labor. McBride and his sons watched a lone red fox jumping in the hayfield, pouncing for mice with devilish glee. The people came to call this place McBride's Slashings, after the acres they wrestled for dominion, but the names can be forgotten. Trees can reclaim the fields, maps can burn, courthouse deeds can be painted in the wondrous colors of mold.

In the distance, among the frailing waves of grain, the fox's red tail flickered like the birth of a field-fire. The two young men rose from their haunches, taking up their guns to go out and make it worth something, for from their visitors, they took their lessons.

MATES

THE DEER'S HAUNCH SHIVERED IN THE crosshairs. The hide was winter's gray, and the air didn't feel like November. Cold had come early this year, indifferent as the sharpest scythe.

The haunch moved: a doe. Crosshairs swung after.

Revealing the white underthroat that men seldom see, she balanced artfully on hind legs to pluck the wine-dark fruit hanging in the sumac. Her weight tugged off a fist of berries. Each bone-colored limb quivered in the air. Snow sifted down, snow that would be gone by noon.

Sull Mercer eased the .270 into the cleft of his shoulder and took a rest off one knee. His rifle was scoped with a 3x9 Leupold—an expensive piece of equipment—but Sull would have told you it was anything but a luxury. It found the tuck behind the doe's shoulder, that corridor to heart and lung. When she passed into a notch between shagbarks, a chance would flicker. For three decades now, this rifle had been comfort in his hands—the bolt worn smooth of its checkering, the burled walnut dark with weather and age. A twig popped under his shifting heel. No more than the crack of a finch's bone.

The doe stamped a foot. Moments ticked by. She performed an elaborate dance, dropping her head and bobbing it up, then back down again and on and on, ears switching, goading him to move. She was an old doe, barren now, and knew threat by its first name. If the flag of Sull's face rustled in the greenbriers, she'd crash through the brush. He held.

His wife craved the liver. He pictured the doe bearing it to them in her body, a gift.

She took a step, with a slight slew-footed twist of the foreleg. Sull flinched. He knew this deer! Before his son Eric had gone to the penitentiary, Sull helped stalk her at the abandoned quarry, where she'd bedded with a lone fawn. This dance had saved her life then. Eric was young, impatient. He tossed four careening shots as she ran. A wild clean miss, each one. It was everything Sull told him not to do. All three sons had learned it over the years, a psalm: *One cartridge, one kill. The rest is just slop.* In a voice chilly as spring water, Sull had told him, "You work that bolt like an automatic, don't you? Maybe they drafted the wrong one of you."

Eric didn't speak to him after that. It made Sull bite his lip to think it now. But Sull was calm, even as the doe's stormy eyes slid over his body. He'd killed enough deer to hang every hook in a slaughterhouse, and few things excited him now that his children had gone on. The doe put forth a tentative hoof. The crosshairs leapt and a peal of thunder rattled the woods. Wrens vanished from the sumac into that pure balance: receding echoes, an expanding silence.

A fox had taken five of the Rockinghams Sull raised as a crib against lean winter months. They didn't need the hens, really, with the grocery selling them on the cheap, but he nursed their absence like a blister. The thought of a deer hanging—the lactic acid breaking down, the meat's surface curing to a glossy black rind—made him feel confident in his sustenance.

She didn't travel a yard. The bullet had ripped a wet socket through the heart, and the doe collapsed as if her knees had turned to stove ash. Hind legs kicked convulsively, brooming leaves. Sull kept the scope on her as she seized, then thumbed on the safety when death was sure. Approaching, he checked his pocket for the familiar heft of the Schrade. She was hoary with age across the muzzle and shanks. Nicked, scalloped hooves. A fleeting regret: perhaps he should have killed something tender and young. Her muskiness drifted up to him. The body had a catatonic beauty, a still life. The exit wound, a slight red star, told a perfect shot. Shame no one else would see it. Marion would be happy for the liver, though, and maybe the twins would come down from Michigan to hunt Thanksgiving. After their discharges, Joel first and Jeffrey eight months later, they had found good union jobs in an auto plant and married Midwestern women about as quick as boys can find them. Sull and Marion couldn't blame them. Anyone here with any ambition did the same. *Ambition*, they all said, chewing the word.

Sull was pleased and sad the hunt had ended so early, but it would give him time that evening to open the gilt-edged King James and glean its comfort. But the day itself comforted more. A windless cold, the kind that keens the senses and brings a gift of ice to the lungs. He'd have Marion write about the doe in her letter to Eric. After pulling the doe onto a rotten quilt of snow, Sull shucked gloves and jacket and rolled his sleeves. He gutted as if he were trying to ration motion itself. After years of fieldwork, he performed the ritual with surgical efficiency. The heart belched a ragged last beat. He fished out a rope, tied it round her neck, and quartered uphill. Innards left her body with a wet sigh and steamed. Arms gloved in blood, he plucked leaves off her eyes and mouth and smoothed the fur tenderly. Pooling blood began to congeal and maroon. He rubbed snow on his knife and hands. Foxes would find the gut-pile and stick their muzzles into the rich leavings, all the way up to their eyeballs. They would eat the pink snow itself. Then buzzards, considerately stripping earth of the dead.

Dragging the body, he thought of his hens. No tracks printed on the raked earth, no cabbage-sized hole marring the drywall. After three nights yawning with a snake-charmer .410 in his arms, Sull dug the rusty leg-hold traps out of the attic, a pair of size two double-coilsprings and a big Newhouse Three. The hinges ached. With a steel brush, he brought iron back to life and nursed the springs with beeswax in the worst, twangiest spots. He baited them with meat scraps, which shriveled untouched till they resembled dried mushrooms. This fox was awful.

A grouse flushed from an upturned washing machine. Snow gave way to leaves and a dump where greenbrier stitched the work of generations: bald tires and log-chains rusted into solid piles, gallon jugs and stripped sedans. He skidded the deer onto a logging road that died into the slope behind his house. Pausing to catch his breath, he saw the silhouette of a great dark hawk that lit on the electric pole near the drive. It shook its vast wings of parasites and tucked them back. Sull's face grew hot. Dead hens. No tracks. He'd been a fool.

He dropped the rope and leaned into his shot. When he pulled the trigger, the hawk stiffened and fell. Sull ran with an old man's jauntiness and found it buckling in the gravel. Scaly, cadmium talons gripped for empty air like palsied hands. Guard feathers obscured the chest, but his bullet had torn a red void out its back. A wing flapped. Turning the bird over with his boot, he saw it was a mature bald eagle. He grinned. It died then.

With a dull hammer, Sull nailed the eagle to the side of the barn, a derelict creamery, to ward off other predators. The parchment skull gave easily under the sixteen-penny nail, its honed point shining, and the sharp wedge of beak caved to the hammer-blow. He stood back to admire his handiwork. The

MATTHEW NEILL NULL

screen door cracked in its keeper. The pitcher in Marion's hand was lacy with suds. "You scared me," she said, with a pinched look. "I dropped a dish."

"Sorry. I seen this on the light-pole. I shot him. Weren't no fox. An eagle!" Breathing hard, he wiped his smiling face on a shoulder. Sweat had turned his gray hair the dark, wet sheen of merchant pig-iron.

"You allowed doing that?" she asked.

"Yeah I am," he said curtly. He spoke through a fixed smile, as he tended to do when flustered. He'd expected her to beam. "Shot us a doe. She'll eat good. Hose in the garage?"

"Is where it always is. You remember the liver?"

"Shit."

She flinched at the word. He'd left the tender organ buried in the gut-pile like a precious coin. Marion's favorite part, if a tad rich for his palate. She had reminded him of it three times. He picked shyly at his hammer-welted fingers. Blood had troughed blackly in the folds of knuckles.

"Want me to fetch it?" Though he knew crows would be playing rowdy by now.

She shaded her face, her pretty gray eyes. "No, no. It's alright."

"I want to," he said, coloring. He was angry at himself, and angry at her. "I'll run up."

"Too late anyhow."

"You want me to shoot another?"

"No. Well, maybe later this year. I'd hate to have one killed just for the liver."

"We'll get us one when the twins come. Here, come take a look at this old boy."

The eagle was huge. Marion put a tentative finger to the claws. A train of blood eased down the whitewashed boards, the fierce yellow gleam draining from its iris. Sull and Marion heard a shrill cry breaking in two parts, then three. The eagle's mate was banking to the clouds above Fenwick Mountain. As she climbed updrafts on stiff wingbeats, the circle she made grew and grew, expanding like a pupil to the shifting of light.

Eric couldn't come home. "They're only allowed a furlough if a close relative dies," the warden had told them. "That's state policy. Mother, father, brother, sister, son, or daughter, God forbid. Guard escorts them the morning of the funeral and brings them back that afternoon. I can tell you're good church kind of people and I hate telling it to you, but it's true."

In the first riot, the warden turned off power and water for ten days. When light shined again, the prisoners were made to carry dead men to the corner of the yard. It was three hundred fifty-two and a half feet long, eighty-two and a half feet wide, and Sull's son knew every inch. Eric's crew buried four unclaimed men with crosshairs chasing them like horseflies, rifles leaning from gothic battlements.

Yet Sull had things to give thanks for. Carter and Reed Mc-Culloch would soon come for buck season, taking the same stands they did every year. The hollow where he shot the doe was only half a mile from his house. A low ridge off Fenwick Mountain, footed there like a foal to its mare. Coastal Timber owned the thousand-acre tract, letting oaks grow upward to the saw, but Sull knew the land better than any company surveyor. He'd learned the place from his father and Uncle Aubrey, memorizing trees as one does a prayer book. Despite the yellow POSTED signs, no one meddled with him there, at least not for now, though he did come across others, like the young grouse-hunter working his brace of bird dogs like a currycomb through the rough pelt of mountainside. What could he say? Was it his place to run people off? He feared others. On a whim, they could take the place away from him, make it theirs. There would be no room for him, or those like him.

Marion reminded him of the McCullochs' visit at supper, after they had speculated on the habits of eagles. Sull Mercer and snaggletoothed Carter McCulloch sprung from the same tintype great-grandmother, a mad seamstress from Anthem who wore a celluloid visor against the sun and a human molar set in a ring—she said it belonged to the jawbone of Thomas Jefferson. Beyond blood, Carter was Sull's best and oldest friend. In their youth, they had been the most talented poachers of their generation, jacklighting bucks, exploding trout streams with bottles of carbolic acid and netting the astonished catch as they bobbed to the surface, air bladders ruptured. One Veterans Day they creeled 123 native brook trout from Whitehorse Run. The legal limit was six. Fried them popping with ramps and potatoes and ate them from the skillet like smelt, bone and eye and all, till the boys passed out gorged and greasy round the fire-ring. Half the fish they left for raccoons to have a holiday. Sull always laughed to his wife how goofy it was Carter grew up to be a game warden. What's writ for you in the Book of Life, you never know.

"Yes, the McCullochs are good people," Sull told her, "but they're not sons, they're not blood in that sort of way." Marion said it was too bad their own boys couldn't find good jobs around here like Reed did, or Carter did before him.

Sull and Marion argued after that. But he did remember to make a promised phone call.

Reed McCulloch, Carter's boy, coasted into the drive the next morning in his dime-bright Chevy. He was a young lawyer, and all the country people did business through him. When Eric got in trouble, Reed had found the Mercers a fine criminal lawyer, though it did them no good. No one could have talked judge and jury out of a Moundsville sentence for their son.

Sull was welding a broken bed-frame for the boy. He wondered how the hell you could break a thing like that, but when Reed's fiancée climbed out of the truck, he had a pretty good notion. "Hey there, who's this good-looking woman you brung me?"

Reed grinned. "Miranda, this is Uncle Sull. He's the last of the mountaineers."

"Pleasure to meet you," she said, tipping her face to Sull in a way that made him embarrassed for the green crescents of his fingernails, the licks of uncombed hair curling out from under his oil-stained cap. She came from Marshall County, where the penitentiary was, and her voice was like a Yankee's, crisp and clipped.

Sull decided not to offer his hand. He gave her a little wave. "Pleased to meet you, miss." Sull turned to Reed. "How much you paying her?"

She cuffed Sull's arm and laughed. Fretful hens were milling by their feet.

Reed said, "I'm paying with a new house, by all accounts. We closed on some acreage near the gorge yesterday. Just a speck by the National Forest."

"Oh yeah? How many acres?"

Reed looked away, to the broken quartzite peak of Fenwick Mountain. The other eagle, maybe? Instinctively, Sull followed his gaze. The mountain still held snow, which had melted off in the valley. Reed tucked his tongue into a cheek. "Three hundred and forty," he said.

"That's more than a speck, that's awful goodly land. Know how little I got here?"

"I've hunted every inch of it." Reed was referring to the Coastal Timber property.

Sull winked at Miranda. "Don't be too impressed. That's a bad habit of his, exaggeration. Not so many inches in this place as he'd lead you to believe. He ever tell you a thing like that?"

She blushed. "Don't mind me," Sull told her. "Old men just talks like that."

Reed laughed. "I'd like for you to see the place. Maybe Dad can bring you out."

"We'll do it. I haven't seen him out and about lately."

"We're stopping by Mom's on the way home. I'll tell him to come see you."

"Suppose you want that bed-frame."

"Here, I'll help you."

While they carried the frame from the shop, Marion stepped out to meet Miranda. When the women weren't looking, Reed slipped his father's friend a folded twenty-dollar bill. Sull tucked it into his watchpocket. Reed asked, "Are the twins hunting with us this year?"

"'Deed I don't know. Say it depends on their vacation. Joel had him a baby this spring."

"I hope they come. It's been a couple years."

"GM works them pretty hard up there."

Marion was giving Miranda an apron full of late apples that shined as if they'd been lacquered. Side-by-side, the pair struck Sull about as unalike as women can be, though he knew it wasn't fair to think that way. One night he and Marion heard Eric talking on the phone in the living room when he came home drunk. "If that redneck slut looks at me like that one more time, I'll put her eyes out. I swear to God, I'll do it with my own hands." Eric was talking about his girlfriend. They'd never heard him so much as cuss. In the twilight of their room, Sull felt Marion's body stiffen then shiver beside him, but she said nothing.

As he walked with Reed McCulloch, who would Marion compare him to?

Marion touched the girl's arm, telling tales. Miranda laughed in an easy way. She seemed graceful and confident, not like the sort of women his sons brought around.

Sull asked, "She a nice girl, Reed?"

"Oh yeah. She's from a good family."

"We're happy for you. Real happy. You be careful, though. You don't want one rides you too hard, you know what I mean?"

Miranda was complimenting Marion on the way she painted the doors and shutters teal in the summer. Then she laughed at the goats, the color of charcoal and chalk, that had wandered over to gaze at her with their fancy hell-colored eyes. "Things are a nuisance," Marion said. "Don't get near or they'll devil you, they'll chew the hem of your dress."

The men heaved the bed-frame into the Chevy. Sull's corner nicked the paint. He saw Reed grimace, but the boy quickly swept it from his face. In the open barn, the doe hung by the neck, dribbling blood into a pan and twisting on the rope. They walked to the kennel so Reed could say hello to his old friends, Sull's black and tans: Fife and Drum, Ring and Train, and Sharky, the crip. They stood bawling on hind legs, nails hooking on the hexagonal wire-mesh. They licked Reed's fingers through the wire. Like all hunting packs, they seemed one feint, one animal.

"What in the hell is that?"

"It kept killing chickens. Got five before I took it out of commission."

"That's a bald eagle!"

"No shit?" said Sull, a wicked smirk ratcheting his face tighter and tighter. "Thought about getting me a bird book."

"Eagles are federally protected now. You could get in big trouble."

"How big?"

"A few thousand dollars. Maybe jail time."

Sull chased the thought from the air with his fingers. "Ain't seen no warrant."

"Somebody could call you in on it."

"Like who?" Sull's one neighbor in sight was a VFW man with a watery heart and a shuddering walk. He never left the house in cold months.

"I'm just warning you, deer-slayer."

"Thanks for the warning. Now you tell your old Dad I told him what he could do with himself, if you get what I'm saying."

"Ha! I'll tell it to Mom, too."

"You tell Letha we love her."

After they left, Marion said maybe he should pitch that eagle over the hill. Sull said no, not at all, it would warn the other away from the yard.

An hour later, the eagle's mate appeared as a distant mote in the sky. She haunted the farm, carving the air with her hooked beak, her metronome wings beating time. Greater in span than the one he'd killed, she perched confidently in the walnut or watched him from the barn's apex, like a weathervane. When Sull stepped into sight, she'd fly from his gun.

Around one o'clock, she took a Rockingham hen with the sound of a handclap. Sull tossed open the door, fumbling a shell into the breech, but only managed to throw a worthless blast when she was well out of shotgun range. His finger caught on the trigger guard. The cut burned as blood ran from his knuckles and into the creases of skin. Hens cowered under the porch, reassuring one another with soft, gurgling clucks.

The door cracked when he punched it.

He spent the next hours shut up in the shop. In the slack of the year, he invented chores: tend the chainsaw, fool with equipment, make it better. Keep animals alive, read the almanac, plan another year. Whet knives for melons and shoats, pump antifreeze, harvest bills and army pension from the junk mail. He tucked his jeans into rubber shitkickers to go check the spring.

Stepping into sunlight, he read the sky for the eagle's mate but saw nothing. He fed brass cartridges into the .270 and took up a crowbar. The wind gleaned tears from his eyes.

He reached the fading field-road where a meager little run sluiced the pasture, just enough water to wet the tongues of cattle.

A pair of Angus lowed as he approached. Sull hollered, "How you doing, girls? Your old Dad's here to love you." The water was shallow this time of year, so half a century ago his Uncle Aubrey had hauled a yellowing clawfoot bathtub there in an oxcart. An iron pipe hammered into a hillside spring kept it full, but in cold months, Sull had to chip ice twice a day. It splintered under the crack of metal, and his Angus shouldered forward to taste the wealth that bloomed from the blow. He gave them kindly smacks on their haunches as they dipped. This run used to be a pure trout stream, but a thousand sucking hooves had chopped it to a muddy ditch. Sull imagined wild brook trout, cold and firm in the fast, healthy current, buried in the water like ingots of precious metal. They hold fast to the bank, laurel-green with bellies of coal-fire. Wilder colors than you'd dare imagine on your own. Stock had destroyed the run—to be truthful, the Mercers had—and silky mud rose off the bottom in slow veils where the Angus dropped their hooves. Do rivers have ghosts? Do trout swim the air?

Coming home, Sull saw her perched on the light-pole. The crowbar fell with a muted clatter. The eagle lifted her hooded eyes. The bullet missed, and she floated unharmed, at a leisurely clip, up Fenwick Mountain. Sull muttered a blasphemy under his breath, then asked God to forgive him.

Marion had taken their coughing Buick to Corinth for groceries and to visit their daughter, June, a bank teller who never gave them a speck of trouble. Sull never felt right when Marion was gone. The mildest bite of food would make his stomach ache and brim. When he was in the army, her letters promised the happiest life when he returned, and he let himself believe. They were married by a justice of the peace and moved here that same afternoon. The first week, he knew something was wrong. Before long, Marion was moving back to her mother's home for two or three months at a time. Sull's father had said, "Some women just does that. When you fill her belly, she'll quit," and though his father managed to be wrong about nearly all else in life, he was right on this. Thank God they had children. Maybe she'd like to go to her mother's even now, but her mother was twenty years gone.

As Sull kicked off his boots, the phone began to clatter in its cradle. Through twenty minutes of pleasantries, he knew from the edge in Carter McCulloch's voice what the man wanted to say. His game warden voice. Reed must have told him. They didn't keep a thing from one another. Finally, Sull asked, "You calling about that stupid bird, right?"

"It's illegal. Real illegal."

"Remember when you jump-shot that hoot owl? I about shit. I'll never forget the look on your face. Said you thought it was a grouse. Biggest grouse I ever seen."

"That was thirty years ago, bud."

"So?"

"Throw it in the woods," Carter said. "Don't keep a claw. Don't keep a feather. You can't have any part of it. Serious this time."

"What if I tell people it's roadkilled?"

"Throw it out, Sull. Do it for me, alright?"

"Alright, Mother Hubbard. When you coming out?"

"Not soon, I hate to say. Getting ready for rifle, got a couple new guys on staff."

"Best see you before Thanksgiving."

"You will," Carter said. "I got to sight-in that 7mm Reed got me."

"Yes, sure. Don't be a stranger."

"I won't."

The next morning, Sull heard a six-cylinder whining up the road. He stepped out to find Carter ambling up the walk in his olive uniform. The state truck gleamed behind him. "Look here, it's old tin-star in the flesh. I thought the outlaws and vandals was the end of you."

"How you doing, Sull?"

"Been awhile."

"Too long."

"Yes, too long."

Carter stepped onto the porch and grinned with that funny, pinched leer of his, as if the left corner of his mouth had been darned up with a stitch. Sull cleaned a finger of tobacco off his palate and slung it into the yard. They shook hands with grips of iron, as men can who have come of age together. Sull said, "That Georgia corn-cracker they want to elect has your name."

"Yeah. I seen that."

"You cousins?"

The smile drifted from Carter's face. "I let you off the hook and now you throw it in my face." Carter took off his broad-brimmed felt hat, which was greening with moisture. With his bald spot showing, he'd aged ten years in a breath. He used the hat to point at the barn, where the bedraggled eagle was still shedding wing feathers. "Throw it in front of God and everybody."

Sull scratched the back of his hand, near a russet birthmark. "Nobody comes out here."

"I ask you to do a simple thing and you lie to me. Lie right into the damn phone," Carter said, slapping his thigh in cadence each time he said *lie*.

"I told you not to worry about it."

"Yeah?"

"I'll say it again. Don't worry about it. I know what I done."

"Well, I'm kindly worried, seeing how it's kindly my ass you put on the line. You want me to write you up? You really want to go to Anthem? That's a federal judge. That local boy shit don't cut it up there. He don't care who you're related to. He's never even pissed on grass."

Eric had wanted to be a game warden, but he had mild epilepsy, weak eyesight, and couldn't even pass the pistol test. Sull hated to think about it. His own son. Because of the epilepsy, Eric couldn't get his CDL, though a hack-and-mend doctor had offered to fix the papers for two hundred dollars. Sull slammed the office door, hard enough to crack the frosted glass.

"I'm not allowed to protect what I got? Just let anything walk in here and take it?"

Carter made a show of sighing. "I don't make the rules, I just enforce them. I took an oath."

"Horseshit."

"I take it serious. You don't believe it, but I do."

"You took it real serious when I slid you some of that deer across the table last year. I believe you said it was pretty good."

Carter blushed. "I didn't know where it come from. We was drinking."

"You knew I shot it out of season. Believe you pardoned me in front of the whole table."

"You know what the trouble is? I let the piddly shit slide, cause I'm from here, I know how it is. Been doing it twenty-six year now. But you know what? That just bites you on the ass. You're good to people and they go bragging on what they get over on you. But I know the tricks. They don't get shit over on me. Swear to God, you all think you own the place."

Sull opened his arms. "We do own the place. Look around you. This is ours," he said, tapping his sternum with two worn fingers the color of boot leather. "When that judge has come and gone we'll be here holding the bag. We're on our own out here, bud."

"Aw, quit poor-mouthing."

"They get the timber and the coal and the votes and they wash their hands of us. Law, law, law. Nobody holds them to the law."

"That's not how it is," Carter said, working himself up to his full six feet. He put his hat back on. "That's not how it is at all."

Sull didn't hear him. "Where's the justice in that? Did you put your hand on the Bible and swear to bother your own people?"

"Look—"

"No, you look. All your eyes behold is God's and He give it to us so we can scratch our way through. I'm doing it. Damn it, you know I'm right."

Carter shook his head. "The law is the law. Today. You got to take it down today."

Boots cocked on the rail, Sull waited an hour. Finally, he traded his shotgun for a spade and hefted the burlap sack. It was bound with baling twine.

Cresting the hill, he happened upon the family cemetery among the trees, where oaks gave way to sullen pines. They had quit the place a generation back because of the encroaching woods and a newfound desire among the more religious ones to rest in churchyards, which would guarantee, they said, the Mercers would be parsed from the heathens in the final reckoning. The Indian tribes knew better than to tend this marginal soil, but these white people had been here a long time, the first to drag up new ground from the Alleghenies. The Mercers stopped here, finally, because it was the first place no one made them leave. Their history was tangible as stone. They could put it in their mouths and break their teeth bloody on it. Sull could kneel and mumble his broken teeth onto the ground.

The gravestones listed toward the horizon and whispered archaic demise: hydrophobia and crib death, scarlatina and Spanish flu. A lone obelisk rose, a bony finger marking the path to heaven. The stones were badly in need of mending, cleft by ice and water and eaten through with the soft persistent teeth of lichen. Some names were beyond weathered, illegible now, never again to bear witness or be muttered aloud. Sull felt guilty for this, yet could think of no solution for the matter of time. Those from the last century lacked any alphabet but the nicks and wormtrails of old letters. Many children, three to an adult. Sull paused to run his fingers over vanishing names of great-aunts and uncles who had returned to the earth. Grievous times. Three gone in 1918, two in 1920, the year between one of respite. Sull remembered a skipping rhyme his mother used to hum around the house: *I had a little bird, her name was Enza, I opened up the window, and in-flew-Enza!*

He pushed aside thick vines that unfurled from above and drooped late bunches of wild grape the size of single-ought buck. His father wanted to be buried here, but Sull let his half-sisters make the final decision; he reasoned that women brought men into the world and should have the final say in their going. Sull's father should rest in the Anthem Cemetery, they said, beside their mother, India, his second wife. In this way, Sull let himself defy his father's wish. It had galled him for a decade now. He promised to return on Memorial Day. Marion would bring flowers. Carter, too. Maybe Reed and Miranda, show them where their people came from.

Sull walked a few paces downhill from the cemetery, figuring this as good a spot as any. His spade rasped in the cold ground. Two feet down, splinters of ice sparkled in the dirt. He turned a good-sized furrow and planted the sack with the eagle in it. Ten pounds of flesh? Twelve? A greasy sweat broke on his brow, and he swabbed it with a bandanna. His father trapped foxes and shot raptors back when you could make a dollar that way, trading pelts and filling bounties for the state. Whole families took part in the commerce, with stiff piles of foxes, hawks, eagles — eagles! — owls, coyotes, raccoons, bears, and bobcats on the fly-swarmed road-side. Government men and fur traders came every other week with a fat wad of bills that bought many a man groceries, even through the Depression, and left in gore-slaked buckboard wagons, the planks leathery with dry blood. Scrawny children clapped and danced and bought oranges at the store. A thick red fox pelt brought the best money, hide stretched like a six-pointed star across the barn siding, a nail in each black-socked foot, the tail, the limp nose, for everyone up and down the road to see. That and the meager ground and the CCC kept them alive.

The hole could use another foot or dogs might get at it. He set the eagle aside and bit into the earth once again. There he turned up a narrow mineral, the color of sun-warmed cream.

He held it to his eye. No rock, no arrowhead. It was a finger-bone, and there another. Sull turned the bone in his hand. The tiny gravestone had rolled downhill, but here was a child's grave he had opened, the grave of an aunt or uncle or cousin. A shiver climbed him. He stuffed the eagle into the hole with his boot and covered it, packing the mound with harsh slaps of the spade. His throat dry as cinders. He tried not to cry, and failed.

At home that night, he read the Old Testament's black verses and the red of the New. What does God think of a man who defiles his family's ground? Would Sull be punished? When he thought of God, he imagined a workingman with callused hands, an eye for detail, and a firm, unyielding love that demanded much. Sull wondered if God thought of him at all.

Marion was watching a television special on a distant country strewn with trash and palms. Brown children tumbled about the legs of US soldiers. Wading endless words, Sull asked her to turn off the television, and she did. Quietly, she rose and stoked a fire in the potbelly stove with kindling and newsprint. Oily paper flared, yellow tongues and antlers of flame, erasing deaths and marriages and auto sales. Watching it burn, Sull knew his punishment had already come. It stunned him. Was God wise and conniving that way, as tricky as any politician? Shaken, Sull closed the Bible and set it aside.

Marion said, "I dreamt about Eric last night."

"Did you?"

"It was a good dream."

"That's good," he said. "I'm glad you did."

Marion set two places at the table, keeping her back turned to hide the crimped, mournful smile on her face, and Sull remembered the intricate route to the penitentiary, way up in the northern panhandle: Highway 33, Pigeon Run Road, Fallen Timber Road, Route 250, Route 7, Route 2. A three-hour trip, one way. The warden had Eric setting pillars in the penitentiary's coal mine. Before the trial, the lawyer had said that if Eric pleaded guilty, the judge might send him to the prison farm at Huttonsville, where he could live among the less violent and learn a skill. It was only forty minutes away, no more than a Sunday drive. As they sat on the hard benches of the Cheat County courthouse, Sull bowed his head and listened to Marion chanting her prayer: *Oh God, I ask nothing else of You. Please keep him safe.* The bailiff touched her shoulder.

After dinner, they sat on the porch. The sun hunkered behind Fenwick Mountain. Marion asked if he'd like a cup of coffee. "Sull. I asked you a question."

"What now?"

"You want you some coffee?"

"I like that," he said, watching smoke spiral from the neighbor's chimney. A wasted Chevy, with FARM USE ONLY sprayed on both doors to avoid the fifteen-dollar tag fee, stood dormant in the drive. Mice nested on the engine block. Everything fallow.

Marion set a steaming mug at his side and squeezed his shoulder. Sull thanked her. She kept standing there, so he looked up into her face, at her weak chin, at the pretty ridge of cheekbone, at the white beginnings of a cataract in her left eye.

"You was a good dad to them," she said. "Real good. No one could have done better. It weren't right of me to blame you."

Marion had never said such a thing, but over the last few years, Sull felt the silent accusation radiate like heat from her skin. His sons hadn't considered their birthright—this hard land—worth having. They scattered into the world. The failure must be his.

He saw the muscles of her cheek begin to shiver. If Marion started at it, he would, too. She knew this and drifted inside. He set his jaw. He couldn't again, not today. Lightheaded, he looked around for something solid to touch.

For a long while, he sat on the steps and sharpened the chainsaw blade with a round file, dipping it in bar-and-chain oil and raking it over each tooth with sleek, grating sounds. He lost himself in the rhythm of labor. A victory over tears is a small thing, but it was his. The sky went from indigo to blackness, and he saw nothing ominous in it, nothing but cold stars wheeling in their course, a course determined by the same firm hand he hoped was guiding his own. But satellites, too, crossed the sky in sly, winking arcs. Sull knew that. He could not let himself be confounded. He went inside, to sleep by his wife.

By the first week of December, he couldn't stand it anymore. He'd held his fire for a month now, and all the hens were gone. When the eagle's mate flew to an ivory treetop on the hogback ridge, near the graveyard, Sull didn't take down his .270. He lifted the chainsaw, a good Stihl, and went tramping through ankle-deep snow.

Sull flushed the eagle from her nest, which was large as a raft and took up the entire crown. The size and scope amazed him, deep with dead white branches. Why hadn't he come here before? He slapped the red oak to test it. His breath, a silver hush.

With a yank of the ripcord, the chainsaw snarled to life, and Sull bit into the bole, giving it a felling notch worthy of timber country. He goosed the saw to a steady, ravenous whine. When the oak finally gave — so fast and so slow, like hot drizzling molasses — it went crashing, loud and brazen, as if it had craved the earth for years and years. He hit the kill switch. Despite the great ripping clots of grapevine and growth, the eagle's nest had held firm in its rigging, but Sull knew it was worthless here on the ground. He stood on the stump till the light grain oxidized, like the bite out of an apple. It had been a great oak, the father of thousands. Sull couldn't wrap his arms around it, for he'd tried once. He knelt and with the tip of his Schrade counted the seasons of the tree, marking years of mast and dry, fire and flood. He watched the sky and saw nothing but clouds traveling with black bellyfuls of snow. Sull had expected to feel guilty, for he hated cutting a red oak, his favorite kind for its bounty of acorns, but a smile came and cracked his face. They'd had a nice Thanksgiving with their daughter's family, Christmas was on its way, and he had deer-meat wrapped in butcher paper. He shot a decent six-point on the third day of buck season, and Reed an even nicer one. He had good health. Marion, too. Perhaps they could take a train to Flint, visit the twins.

Shrieking above.

He glanced up at the sky's gray vault and saw the eagle's mate pulling herself upward, flying over the backbone of Fenwick Mountain. Sull watched till she was small as a chickenhawk, small as a period, then small as nothing at all.

Smiling, he began to descend the hillside at a good clip, picking his way through briars on a hoof-beaten trail. One of the deer had been a huge buck that survived rifle season against all odds. The marks of its splayed hooves and dewclaws were tamped into the earth so deeply they dwarfed the tracks of does, fawns, lesser bucks. Maybe Sull would find the shed antlers come February. He settled on his haunches and put bare fingers to one of the icy prints, tracing its dimensions. The cold soothed his ungloved hand. Then he heard a familiar cry.

The smile seeped from his face. Once again, the mate banked against the ridgeline, gliding back in his direction, gliding effortlessly, like she could do it forever.

NATURAL RESOURCES

BEARS HAD BEEN SEEN ON THE road. Black bears, young males thrown out the den, nipped at by their mothers, romping over the green drop cloth of spring. They tore up the last worm fences in that county—those relics of another life, 1860, 1870—and raked the wood for termites. They scared cows and old men picking up trash along the road. Too early, the young males tried mounting sow bears, to make more of their perfect selves. When bitten hard and warned back, they looked joyous even then. So happy to be alive. After two hundred years of decline, they were managing an upswing. A new era had come.

When the population dropped to less than five hundred statewide, the legislature had responded. It closed entire counties to bear hunting, over the protests of farmers and sportsmen; voided the bounty system; banned hounds; tripled the number of game wardens. It established the Cranberry Wilderness—a fifty-thousand-acre swatch of mountains—and made it a sanctuary. This was public land, bought back from timber companies when it was nothing but fire-scarred leavings. No vehicles allowed. No guns.

Two decades passed. Black bears took to this stony land and, to everyone's surprise, other ruined places. They found the first-generation strip mines, exhausted of coal, the mountains carved down to nubs and benches and abandoned like botched pieces of pottery. The strip mines grew lush with exotic plants the coal companies seeded there to stop the entire county from sloughing downhill in wet plates. By the time the legislature made it law to use native plants for mine reclamation, there was little left to reclaim. Autumn olive and Japanese rose overwhelmed everything, so tough and spry the worst winds couldn't bend them. Tartar honeysuckle matted the slopes in a rich, unnavigable pelt, an otherworldly green, something out of a movie set.

In hindsight, a good place for shy things to lose themselves. When the strip mines filled up like hotels, the bears spilled into an old quarry, then hillside farms gone to briar, to sapling, to forest. They needed just *this much* rock.

They suckled cubs, owned the ridgelines, and toppled apiary boxes in singing clouds of bees. In consternation, in awe, you gazed out the window.

Tuscarora County wasn't used to seeing bears. Many would deny their existence for years to come. Once something had been taken away, it wasn't given back: elk and wolves, mining jobs and cheap gasoline, even a village where the Army Corps of Engineers flooded a valley. So it took a while to believe these visions:

A black cape cracking itself across a midnight road.

Or what looks like a dog, then emphatically is not a dog.

Cubs rolling down a hillside like cannonballs.

Near nightfall on Fridays and Saturdays, a caravan of trucks and cars made its snaking way to the county dump. People lined up at a distance you couldn't call safe. When the natural light turned soft and blue, bears eased off the mountain and sifted through trash. Soft human cries went up. A bear gripped a bowling pin in its mouth. Another savaged a washing machine, rocking it back and forth. Metal cringed. A wealthy store of rotten cabbage was uncovered in all its septic glory.

The show attracted a democratic swath: coal miners and lawyers, nurses and accountants, old and young. This went on for months. If you leaned out the window, a bear would delicately take a lollipop from your pinkly offered palm. *Snap, snap, snap!* went the cameras. You could smell its hide like sour milk.

They called it the poor man's safari. A woman drove there with her children. She wanted a picture of her youngest with a bear; she wanted the child to graze the mystery, as people lift babies from the throng and lean to the president's drifting touch. She took the boy, smeared his hand in honey, and put him out there so sweetness could be licked from his fingers. Moans and nervous laughter from the cars. She had her camera ready. Two bears came loping.

The Department of Health and Human Resources absorbed three children, the county fenced off the dump, the good times were over. And they say this was once home to the happiest bears on earth. *Not only are they giving us their toddlers, they're dipping them in honey first.*

Winter on the way, the bears sequestered themselves deep in the earth. The mountain filled. You thought about them. You had to. You nursed their absence like a missing tooth. Imagine the molasses drip of their sleeping blood, their idling hearts. They're safe from the razor-wire winds that flay you, safe from the leaden days, the country loneliness, the cold stars in the sky. What if the earth shrugs and crushes them in their beds? They won't even know. Which may be the name of bliss.

Far away, the bear question was discussed under flickering fluorescent lights. Time had come for the Department of Natural Resources to draft the new management plan, as it did on the decade. Pens lifted. Legal pads recorded notes, outbursts, muttered asides.

The bear in a cave, its black eye as deep as a well, endless, plunging in blackness deeper than night. Suspecting and unsuspecting of all designs. The pupil focuses, the point of a knife.

Living with them is such a risk. Something must be done. The incident at the dump just goes to show. Can we call a vote? Raise your hands. Higher. The population peaked at twelve thousand. Time to thin them out. A yearly kill of 10% is sustainable. A bear stamp was designed and meted out for tax purposes; estimates of economic impact slavered over. The legislature opened Tuscarora to bear hunting—except for the Cranberry Wilderness, that lone green corner.

You started seeing trucks with bristles of CB antennas and raucous dog-boxes in the back. The first day was a circus. Sound split the quiet places of winter: Cranberry Glades, Hell-for-Certain, Shades-of-Death, Pigeon Mountain. Hounds, reports, radio crackle.

A record harvest. Near the village of Canvas, crowds gathered at the gas station, which had invested in a big tackle scale, the kind harbors use to hoist dead sharks. They had a Hall of Fame, photographs on a corkboard.

Men with arms dipped in blood, and the Chinese merchants there to buy gallbladders, three hundred dollars apiece, green greasy aphrodisiac, casting looks over their shoulders for the warden.

People dug out curling photographs of great-grandpa posing over a dead, darkish thing—a rug maybe? a tarpaulin?—and blew off the dust, taped them to refrigerators. The generations in between were considered—what? a little cowardly?—ones who had forsaken the hunt. The bloodlines of Plott hounds were traced with a care once accorded kings.

You looked forward to December. Walking the ridge, gun in hand, the cold air blooming in your lungs like a tree of ice. Out there among them. One more reason to love this place.

And the biologists were right. In a year, the population recovered.

The Bear Hunters Association called for changes. They proposed an open season in spring and summer. No, they wouldn't shoot the bears, just run their hounds in all that green, for practice. After treeing a bear, they'd let it go free. No harm. Play. God, the sweltering boredom of June. In the country you make your own fun.

The biologists thought the proposal was a joke—with a sinking sensation, they realized the truth. Voters were polled, and thought it a good idea. The legislature responded. The reform was approved 31-3. The DNR director resigned. The governor appointed a new one that day.

Chased three seasons through, the bears couldn't store enough fat for hibernation. They were skinny, mean animals, not the wobbling clowns of seasons past. You got used to seeing hunters out in warm months and muttering into handsets. On the mountain, hounds sang that clean bawling treble, clear as a movie soundtrack. Bears lifted their purpled muzzles from the blackberries, knowing again it was time to run.

Winter mortality on the rise. Cubs aborted in the womb. Old sows crawled back in caves and never came out. The population dropped 65 percent. Biologists pleaded. A response was called for.

The Cranberry Wilderness—the last sanctuary—was opened for business. It had served its purpose. A new era had come.

It took a few malingering years, but that was the end of bears in Tuscarora. Teased endlessly by the dogs, they seemed to fling themselves in front of the guns. Everyone had one of those bleached skulls on the mantel. The orbits were huge. That long, daft grin. You traced it with your thumb. Bone gathered a sleek film of dust and yellowed. Finally, the skulls were stowed away in trunks and drawers among old chattering crockery.

(People cherished the odd sighting and would brag on one for months, for years. A midsized black dog, running, was called a bear. An interesting, dark rock glimpsed from a passing car was called a bear.)

But earth turns, and old ways are reexamined. The insurance companies say there are so many deer, so many wrecks. They have algorithms on their side. Kill more deer. Let all the predators live.

GAULEY SEASON

LABOR DAY. WE COULD HEAR THE bellow and grind from the Route 19 overpass. Below, the river gleamed like a flaw in metal. Leaving the parking lot behind, we billy-goated down the fisherman's trail, one by one, the way all mountain people do. Loud clumps of bees clustered in the fireweed and boneset, and the trail crunched underfoot with cans, condom wrappers, worm containers. A half-buried coal bucket rose from the dirt with a galvanized grin. The laurel hell wove itself into a tunnel, hazy with gnats. There, a busted railroad spike. The smell of river water filled our noses.

Finally, sun spilled through the trees, and we saw Pillow Rock rise as big as a church from the waters. A gaudy lichen of beach towels and bikini tops coated it over. Local women shouted our names. "Happy Labor Day!" When we set foot upon it, the granite seemed to curve to our bare soles, radiating an animal heat. Wolf spiders raced off. We made the top, where Pillow Rock flattened. The river nipped at its base. So much water. The Army Corps of Engineers had uncorked the dam below Summersville Lake. The water churned and gouged at the canyon walls. The Gauley had the reputation of a drowning river, even before the Army Corps wrestled it out of God's control and gave it power.

Upriver, scraps of neon: rafters. Dyes like that don't appear in nature. Their paddles flashed like pikes in the sun.

Rafting brings in millions of taxable dollars a year. The commissioner says it's the best thing to happen to Nicholas County since the Coal Severance Tax. "Coal was king," he says. "Coal *was* king." Men in their twenties and thirties and forties shouldn't stand idle. We who'd lost our mining jobs would work in whitewater, plow that wet furrow. Nice thoughts. Invigorating lies. For our bread, we worked filling stations, timber outfits, hospice care, county schools. The two big successes among us, Chet Mason and Reed Judy, started a welding outfit out of Reed's old, echoing barn. The rafting operators—from Pennsylvania, Oregon, Croatia—brought their own people and did little hiring, until Kelly Bischoff started Class Five. He hired locals. The papers gushed over Kelly. He'd graduated from Panther Creek High School. One of us. Ex-miner. He looked rugged-good and dusky on a brochure, glossy and smiling, holding a paddle. His mother's from Gad.

On Pillow Rock, men and women spoke to one another, casual and cunning. Someone fiddled with a portable radio: white jags of static, the silver keen of a steel guitar. We pried open prescription bottles that carried names other than our own.

Too late for trout fishing, too early for squirrel season—time to sun ourselves like happy rattlesnakes and watch the frolic. Five weeks running in the fall, we did, every Saturday, every Sunday. Opening day was always best. Every few minutes, another raft tumbled over Sweet's Falls and crashed in the shredding whirlpool. After a tense moment, the raft popped up like a cork in a sudsy bucket of beer. We cheered. Agonized faces glanced back, blooming with smiles. They loved us, or the sight of us. They held paddles aloft in pale, white arms and their orange helmets shined. Some claim we don't care about those people, we just take their commerce. Not true. We wonder about their jobs, their towns, their faces, their names.

Kelly Bischoff swore he heard a cash register chime every time they tipped over the falls. I love clientele, he liked to say. Kelly moved between the two worlds, sleek as an otter. He knew us. He knew the rafters. Their names, their faces. He had everything you could want.

"Look, that one's so scared he keeps paddling, not even hitting the water."

Laughter tumbled down the rock. "What a jackass."

"A happy jackass."

"Would you do that?" Chet Mason asked a woman. "Go over the falls?"

"I'd love to scream like that. I never scream like that."

"You hear that, Jason? Sounds like you're not taking care of your husbandly duties."

Reed Judy said, "You pay big money to holler like that. Old Kelly gets two hundred dollars a head. You got to come with a full raft, too. He got *plenty* of rafts."

"How many heads is that?"

"Six in that one, not counting the guide," Chet Mason said. "Slick as a hound's tooth, Kelly is. Course, fall's got to pay for winter, spring, and summer—that's awful heavy math. There he is. That's Class Five, that's Kelly's."

The forty-seventh raft that day. Class Five River-Runners had blue-and-yellow rafts, same colors as the Mountaineers' football team. We were proud of Kelly. After they sealed the Haymaker Mine, he mortgaged his house to start the outfit. Kelly punched out Mayor Cline last year at the festival. Wasn't even drunk.

"Hey, Kelly boy!" We cupped hands around our mouths. "Hey, Kelly!"

He didn't wave back, riding closer on the careening swell. The raft hit at a bad angle. Rocks scraped the wet, blubbery rubber. As it made the lip of the falls—in our bellies, we felt a feathery sympathetic tickle—the raft toppled and shook out bodies.

Quiet. Then the screaming. We bounded down to the water's jagged edge, we tried to tally them, keep the numbers right. Neon tumbling in that gullet of foam, and one frail arm. We reached and missed and cussed ourselves. Reed managed to hook a belt and flopped a man onto the rock.

One disappeared under a boulder for a few sickening moments and shot out the other side. His mouth a hard circle.

With a strong crawl, Kelly led some into a backwater that bristled with logjams and lost paddles. Their heads broke the surface. The current sucked them back.

Kelly and the girl reached up at the same time. Chet Mason was closest. He had one set of hands. He hesitated for a millisecond. He reached for Kelly. "Got you."

A sharp little yelp cut the noise. The girl's helmet disappeared downriver. She was gone.

Young boys slid off the rocks like seals. Tethered with rope, they felt for corpses with their feet; we fished for the dead and walked the living—Kelly and four rafters—up Pillow Rock.

Like nothing had happened, another raft came tippling over the falls. The rafters looked surprised when no one waved. Supplicants, we circled the rock with prepaid cell phones raised in hand, trying for the best reception. Soon an ambulance squalled onto the overpass.

The rescued were quiet now. Hard to believe they'd been wailing, keening, moaning just moments ago. Flogged by the water, they looked haggard—pilgrims who'd been turned back from the country of the drowned. We sat them on beach towels and tried to give them sandwiches. They wore mere bruises and abrasions, but the paramedics nursed them just the same. One kept trying to slip a blood pressure cuff onto them. A blond woman with a tank top and a little too much sun wept and cussed in alternating jags. She did this while wringing water from her hair. She had a stiff, shocked look, like a cat you just threw in a rain barrel.

All the while, more rafts going over.

The survivors sat a ways from Kelly Bischoff. He shivered under a towel, smoking a damp cigarette. He'd stripped off his life jacket and spread it in the sun to dry. His hair, gone gray in patches, had grown out like a hippie's. "Of all the goddamn things," he kept saying.

"How many times you been over the falls?" Reed Judy asked him.

"Three hundred and thirty-one."

"How many times you roll it over on you?"

"Three," he said, pulling on the cigarette. "This was the third. My line was right."

"Looked like you hit it funny."

"My line was right. They let out 3,800 c.f.s. today. Too much river. That," said Kelly, "is God's honest truth." He pressed his ear against the warm granite to draw out the water. He was shaking.

Deputies arrived. They were locals, Hunter Sales and Austin Cogar, young, crewcut, sweating from the hike. Austin stood by the survivors and jotted on a pad. "How old you say she was?"

"I don't know exactly," a rafter said. He was half of a whisper-thin couple who were holding hands on the rock. "She's my friend's daughter. She's in high school."

"Her name's Amanda," Kelly cried. It was sudden, like the fury of a wasp.

Everyone turned to him. Hunter took his arm and tried to lead him aside.

"I know all my clients," Kelly said. He liked calling them by their names. It set things in motion, the tumbling of keys in locks. It made us feel unprivileged.

Hunter asked, "How you doing, Kelly?"

"I been better."

"Turn a boat over, did you?"

"Looks like." Kelly flicked the cigarette into the waters.

"Got good insurance?"

"Damn good. The best."

Hunter told us to give them some room. He lowered his voice and began to question.

"I had one beer," Kelly said, more loudly than he should have. "Washed down my sandwich at lunch. Ask anybody."

The blond woman who'd been wringing her hair spoke up. "You drank three of them," she said, putting a nice little snap on her words. "You put them away fast." She turned to Austin. "He had at least two. Then he sneaked off at lunch with them and—"

Kelly said, "Christina, this is between me and the police. You'll get your turn."

We blushed at the mention of her name, like they'd admitted something sexual. Austin's pen quit scratching.

The blond woman walked over to Kelly. "I have something to say and it's my right."

"Aw, shut up." Then he called her something that made us cringe, even the deputies.

"I'd like to speak to you in private," Austin told her. "All you people go. Come on, get."

She spoke in low tones, her hands fluttering in a crippled-dove dance.

Slowly, we folded our towels but didn't stray far. Kelly sat off to the side like the condemned. Austin talked into a radio pinned to his shirt. "Blond teenager, female, fifteen years of age. Male, forty-three years of age, scar through his eyebrow."

The sun weakened. As the temperature fell, the air began to smell like rain. Deputies said go on home, they didn't need no more statements, though we'd have been proud to give them. The coolers pissed final streams of melt-water, and we made our exodus, one by one. A drizzle fell. Kelly sat in the back of a Crown

Vic cruiser on the overpass, head bowed against the seat in front of him. The drizzle turned to nickel-hard rain, and we heard the blades whapping long before we saw. The helicopter dipped into view. Pterodactyl-ugly, it switched on a searchlight and circled many times. Then it swooped away, called back wherever it came from. The rain turned to roaring curtains. Faintly, the music of rescue disappeared over the ridge.

We found the dead girl wrapped around a bridge abutment at the mouth of Meadow Creek. Her skin was bleached canvas-white by the waters, her eyes pressed shut. For that we were thankful. The rafters aren't supposed to see this stretch of river. It's a world away from Pillow Rock. Here, Meadow Creek sloughed mine-acid into the Gauley after any good rain. It streaked rocks orange and sent a cadmium ribbon of yellowboy unspooling downriver. No fish, no life. The sight of it could make you cry.

"You guys ought to pull on gloves."

We waved off the sheriff and waded in. Hadn't we been raised to treat our hands like tools, our tools like hands? Blue jeans drank up water and darkened.

We built a chain of ourselves then pulled her from the shallows, her hair tangling like eelgrass around hands and arms, refusing to let go. On the green table of pasture, we laid the dead girl's body: coltish, young, trim as a cliff-diver's. An athlete. Her hair twisted into a wet question mark. One leg tucked under her at a funny angle. We pulled down her shirt where it had ridden over her small breasts. Leaves in her hair. "Walnut leaves," someone said.

She looked okay for someone who'd been traveling all night. We wrapped her in plastic and carried her to the road. Sheriff said, "Sure glad Kelly ain't here to see this."

Everyone nodded. It was a solemn occasion. It felt almost holy, to carry a visitor's body in the morning light. None of us had touched one before.

The dead girl's picture found its way into the newspaper, pixilated and gray. She was a high schooler from Bethesda, Maryland, her father a midlevel administrator at the Federal Department of Labor. The mother an ex-wife. Her father was Greg Stallings. We never found his body. We learned the things we did not know. Amanda.

You couldn't have gotten all the leaves out of the dead girl's hair. Not even if you'd sheared it off.

With her death, life changed, a little. Insurance payments were made, rumor and accusation leveled, a dram of ink spilled in the papers. Kelly Bischoff sold his company to a fellow from Connellsville, Pennsylvania, who owned a northern operation on the Youghiogheny and the Cheat. Seventeen of Kelly's people went on unemployment and COBRA, drawing as long as they could. Connellsville had his own guys. No one made big lawsuit money off her death; rafters sign risk papers beforehand, absolving companies of blame. So earth turned, bears scouted their dens, the Army Corps eased their levers down. The river returned to its bed.

We have a tenth of the mining jobs our fathers had.

But Kelly had connections. He found work running a dozer at a strip mine—a fitting job, where he dumped blasted rock into the valley, staunching creeks and gullies with tons of shattered mountaintop. He crafted a featureless flatland where the governor promised malls, industrial parks, golf, chain restaurants. A new round of permits cleared the EPA.

It hurt to see Kelly out of the rafting game. And yes, maybe we're guilty of feeling something special for Kelly, of yoking our fortunes to his. We rooted for him. He showed what our kind could accomplish, if given the chance, in this sly, new world. We could go toe-to-toe, guide with skill, make that money. We were just as good as outsiders, almost equals, we weren't just white mountain trash. The sting of the rafters' uneasy looks when we pumped their gas or offered directions—with a few more Kelly Bischoffs, why, all that would end. Now, nothing.

Then, December. Reed Judy was driving the overpass, making for the tavern at Clendenin Mill, the one that burned last year. A lone figure was washed in the spastic glow of headlights and sucked back into the darkness. Reed pulled over, grit and snow popping under his tires. The man walked up to meet him.

"Can I give you a lift?" Reed asked.

"No, bud. Just taking a look at the river."

Reed heard the Gauley muttering in its dumb winter tongue, but the canyon was black, no river there. He could see the distant warning lights, like foundered stars, where the dam stood low in the sky. Where it divided river from lake. He asked, "You sure? It's blue-cold out."

"Oh, I'm parked down at the turnaround."

It was Kelly.

"Suit yourself," Reed said.

"You Steve's boy? The welder?"

"Yeah."

"You don't look like your mother." Kelly pinned him down with a stare. "Say, you was down there that day. You drug the river. I know you did. Down to Meadow Creek."

Reed panicked, lied. "No," he said. "I don't know what you're talking about."

"Yes, you do. You seen her. Amanda Stallings." Kelly winced. "Did she look okay? God, she was a good girl. She wasn't tore up too bad, was she?"

When Reed didn't answer, Kelly said, "I didn't mean to drown her."

"Course you didn't! Nobody said you did! You don't have to say that."

Kelly said mournfully, "I don't think you understand," and said no more.

Telling it around, Reed itched a particular place on the back of his hand. "Looks like he's aged twenty years, he does."

A month later, Chet saw Kelly on the overpass, hands clamped on the rail. When Chet told the story, he fidgeted and blushed. The sight had shaken him. "I thought about hitting him with the truck and saving the poor son of a bitch from, from—I don't know."

And this was something to say, because in a place with so few people, each life was held precious, everyone was necessary. We saw Kelly again and again that winter. State troopers made him walk the line. He was not drunk. "Kiss my red ass," he cried. "Public right-of-way."

We waited for him to jump.

Every night the dam drew Kelly there. To avoid Route 19, we looped far out of our way, over the crookedy mountain cuts. It hurt too much to see him. But others were vigilant. Every morning, the dam operators of the Army Corps—three lonesome, demoted engineers—scanned the banks and the tailrace with binoculars. They had a pool going as to when Kelly's lifeless body would finally wash up. That sortie out of the powerhouse was the high point of their day. This, after all, was a backwater post among backwaters.

Lyndon Johnson, a president we loved, dedicated Summersville Dam in 1966. Before cutting the ribbon, he made a joke about losing his pocketknife on the way and maybe having the Secret Service throw up a roadblock at the Nicholas County line to find whoever had pocketed his Schrade—too fine a thing to leave just laying around—since he reckoned all West Virginia boys come out of the womb knowing a good knife when they see one. We laughed, and Lyndon took out a bandanna and swabbed at his brow, looking like any worried man.

Acres of virgin concrete. Smooth, vertical. The dam was tall as the face of God. There was nothing else to compare it to. Nothing of such stability, such mass.

The rising waters flooded the village of Gad, home to a store, a filling station, and three hundred people. Eminent domain moved them, even the dead from their graves. (When Kelly stood on the overpass, was he trying to see his mother's village through ninety feet of water? No. He thought only of the girl.) Quietly, later, Gauley Season was created in 1986 by an act of Congress. We had no idea how life would change.

Over unruly rivers and hogbacks, the rectangular Gauley River National Recreation Area was placed like a stencil. It's shaded aquamarine on the maps. Lord—maps and new maps. The rapids had names before the rafters came: Glenmorgan Crossing and Mink Shoals, Gooseneck, Musselshell. They brought a new language: cubic feet per second, high side and chicken line, hydraulic and haystack. They renamed the rapids: Insignificant, Pure Screaming Hell, Junkyard, the Devil's Asshole. Unwritten, our names flew away like thistledown on the wind. Except for Pillow Rock. Our fathers named the rock for the river drivers napping there in the sun, after a punishing morning of busting jams and poling logs downriver. Chet snuck to the foot of the overpass and spray-painted in green neon, PILLOW ROCK AHEAD!!! The last thing a rafter sees before tipping over the falls.

True, the release goes against nature. Gauley Season scours the river, blasting fish from their lies, eyes agog, air bladders ruptured. Even so, Gauley Season brings certain benefits. To atone for the fishery's death, the Department of Natural Resources grows California rainbow trout in hatcheries and drops ten thousand pounds into the canyon by helicopter. The fish have nubby snouts, open ulcers, and tattered fins from rubbing against the concrete raceways. Gray trout, we call them. They taste like they've been stamped out of cat food, but they're free. Come spring, we watch them rain and smack the waters. We cast hooks until every last one's caught and creeled. Sometimes the fish hit the rocks as the helicopter swoops away. Raccoons revel in the blood. They lick their wiry hands, fumbling them in an attitude just like prayer. They rejoice.

"There he is!" an engineer cried. "You win, Sully! He jumped! He finally jumped!"

The others ran out of the powerhouse. He adjusted the parallax of his binoculars in a gloved fist. "Shit. False alarm." What he thought was Kelly was a dead deer twisted—twisting—in sunken willows.

A year passed as they do, quickly, as if in a dream or a coma. We thought of the dead girl and her father less and less, or tried to.

Snow and thaw and rain. Hay was cut in the fields, sallies hatched off the river in lime-and-sulfur clouds, deer grew their velvet crowns. September gleaned a cool wind from the Alleghenies. Labor Day weekend, Pillow Rock gathered its people. We hollered as the Army Corps opened up the gates. Upriver, the beating of ten thousand hooves. We inhaled the water's breath of iron and cedar.

A standing wave broke over Sweet's Falls. The river augered and torqued, a muscular green. Shards of flotsam and jetsam: broken sycamores and garbage bags, bleached timber, a child's tricycle. A water-bloated calf wheeled downriver, eyes blue as heaven.

The air crackled with anticipation. Gas stations and hotels and campgrounds had pitched their banners early: RAFTERS WELCOME, COLD BEER HOT SHOWERS, ASK ABOUT OUR GROUP RATES. This would be a record-breaking season. The *Washington Post* had featured us in their Sunday magazine. The headline read MONTANI SEMPER LIBERI. *West Virginia's secret is out: the number two river in America, number seven in the world. One question remains. Can the whitewater industry save this place?* With the glee of discoverers, they told of the spine-rattling, third-world pike that is Route 19. That wasn't so bad—maybe the Department of Highways would be embarrassed and put in for federal money.

What nettled most were the things they plucked out to describe: junk cars in the river, raggedy bear-hounds jumping in their kennels, crosses at Carnifex Ferry that say GET RIGHT WITH GOD and THERE IS NO WATER IN HELL. All eye-battering, all to be laughed at. Didn't talk about the landing we poured, the oil-and-chip road we laid for their wobbling, overburdened shuttles. "Relax," Mayor Cline said. "Sometimes the fire that cooks your food burns your fingers—you can't bitch." It's dog Latin, the state slogan. We are, it says, always free.

Kelly Bischoff walked in long pants down the fisherman's trail, with a ragged red backpack on.

Pillow Rock went silent.

Work-blackened jeans, dirt in his hair. He peeled off his shirt, shook it of coal dust, and folded it with care. The words *Sweet* and *Sour* were inked in cursive blue over his nipples, with arrows offering up directions. A black panther climbed his bicep, claws drawing stylized blood. A Vietnam mark. He shucked his boots and tucked his cigarettes, wallet, and keys into them. Finally, he pulled out a penknife and snagged off his work pants to the knee.

"You're back among the fold," Reed said to him.

Kelly smiled. "Good to see you all."

"You working that strip job?"

"Yes I am," Kelly said, looking side to side, daring anyone to say a word against it.

"Jesus Was Our Savior, Coal Was Our King. Say, you probably ain't watched from this angle."

Kelly said, "I seen them go over. 1979, it was. Fishing here. Seen Philadelphy Pete Dragan go over Sweet's, back in them too-big green army rafts. Said, Hell, I can do that."

Kelly watched the falls, apart from the rest. What could he read there? The water herded yellow foam into the backwater, a rancid butterfat color, thick enough you could draw your name in it with a fish pole. Where we'd saved four lives last year. Five if we counted Kelly's. If Kelly longed for his old life, he did not say. He just watched the water's horseplay like he could augur it. Maybe he could.

Rafters! We waved and hollered as usual, but Kelly radiated a complex silence. So we grew quiet, not so joyful, and the day grew old. Shadows slithered on the rock. One hundred ninety-seven rafts. Not a one drowned. Clouds came and snuffed our shadows. The air had a little bite to it, so we pulled on sweaters and packed to leave. Slush tipped from coolers, the last orphan beer cracked and drained. Kelly just sat there.

"Them are your people," we said, waving at the last raft.

Kelly shrugged. We gave Reed Judy some hopeful looks, so he hunkered down next to our fallen idol. "You coming? We're going to Bud Shreve's, grill some food. Be fun."

"No, I'll set here awhile." Kelly rummaged around his backpack and found a gray army-surplus blanket. Was he too good for us?

"Alright, bud. You hear about the blind kid up here got bit by the rattlesnake?"

"No, I didn't."

"Least he didn't see it coming."

Kelly smiled and looked at the ground. "That's a good one," he said. Didn't even flinch; there was hope for him yet. But then he whispered something that turned Reed pale and bloodless— and that Reed wouldn't tell about till years later. "You're the one lied about Meadow Creek," Kelly said. "Lied about finding her. Why would you do that to me?"

We left him there as the drawknife of dusk peeled back the world.

•

In heirloom, fifteen-verse ballads, lovers of the drowned flung themselves in, so their bones could frolic and mingle. But Kelly never trucked in old ways. Instead he sat with us.

MATTHEW NEILL NULL

For the rest of the season, Kelly was the first on Pillow Rock and last to go. Word went round he'd slept there through the weekends, under a ragged tent of laurel. "But he looks to be shaving," someone said. Sure enough, he never missed a single raft. He perched there like an osprey. When the maples flared, he began telling stories of the dead girl.

It was hard not to listen. He'd sidle up if you broke away to piss or get another beer. She wanted to be an environmental lawyer, he said. She was an athlete. Once she ran a mile in five minutes and thirty-two seconds, a fluke—her average was six-fifteen. She stayed with her father weekends and summer. She loved dogs. "Oh, who don't?" Chet asked him.

On a coolish day in October, for the first and only time, he spoke to us as a group. Our numbers had trickled, as they do at season's end. Kelly chewed his fingernails, his thumbnail. Sucking the taste from them. Then he spoke.

In Bethesda, the dead girl's home was the size of—he struggled for comparison—of the county courthouse, the one with the statue of Nancy Hart, who seduced her jailer, shot him in his stupid mouth, and brought back a Confederate cavalry to burn the town. Why did our forefathers raise a statue to someone who destroyed them? Our people fought at Carnifex Ferry. Left the trees full of minié balls, as much lead as wood, so they grew hunched and buzzardy under their mineral burden. We sparred and set the boats on fire. They whirled like burning flags in the night and snuffed themselves hissing in the Gauley. Why not a statue to that?

"That's history," Kelly said. "Pull your head out your ass."

"Nothing happens no more. Day in, day out."

He said, "You got no idea."

Well, maybe not. "Idea of what?"

To prove us wrong, Kelly plucked up and spoke—confident now. He explained the last day of his rafting career.

·

When they broke for lunch in the canyon, Kelly offered to lead any stouthearted rafter up Barranshe Run to see the five falls, a stairstep of cataracts up the mountainside.

Hours from drowning, Greg Stallings asked, "Is it far?"

"Little bit. Just follow me, Greg. Anybody else?"

The group sat at a table made of the raft turned turtle. One stood up: the dead girl. Kelly kicked his accent up a notch. "A young thing. Great. You'll lead the pack, Amanda."

"I can take it," she said, with a measure of pluck.

Kelly looked the dead girl over: strong legs, sleek lines. "You can carry her up there on your back," he said to her father, appraising her like a foreign coin. "She still your little girl, right?"

Greg smiled. The others waved them on, faces full of sandwiches and potato salad, bright and ridiculous in their water-sport clothes—chartreuse and pylon orange, same color as the Powerbait we sling to the government trout.

Ascent. The two of them did what Kelly did, clutching the same wet points of rock, the same dry patches of moss for footholds. The trail stitched itself in and out of the creek, where trout danced like Salome in the tannic water. Smell of rotting wood. Squelch and rasp of wet tennis shoes on rock. Kelly explained Barranshe Run was named for a sow black bear that never whelped a single cub. "No one ran their dogs on her, ever, even when she was reelfoot and gray. Don't know why. We kill lots of bears here."

Greg said, "That sounds like a story to me."

"It's just what they say." Kelly knew the rafters were obsessed with fact. They paraded it at him again and again. "Would have been a mercy to kill her."

"That's so callous," the dead girl said.

"Here, you need to stay hydrated. You forget that out here."

She unscrewed the water bottle and took a drink. She wiped her mouth, cocked her head at him.

The trail narrowed. She kept flicking him little looks.

Hands scrabbled for holds. Calves burned with acid. "One more bend," Kelly hollered. There, Great Swallow Falls, thirty foot tall. It sluiced over a mossy lip of stone and sent a misty perpetual rainbow into the air: a fisherman's cast-net frozen mid-throw. The world smelled of cold, rich limestone. Swallows nipped stoneflies. The colored hoop shimmered.

The dead girl showed Kelly how to work the switches on her camera. "Wait, show me again," he said, grinning. She slapped his arm. "Pay attention."

Kelly snapped a picture of father and daughter, perfect for the Internet. "Think that's nice, you ought to see the next one." Each falls more riveting than the last: deeper drop, darker hues, emerald, topaz, Prussian. The swallows piping like bone flutes.

Panting now, Greg said he couldn't go on. He sat on a log, nursing warm spots that promised to blister.

"But the last one's the best," Kelly said, pointing ahead. Now the trail ran vertical, just a thin trough of root and rubble through jagged stone. A deer couldn't run it. The ground called for a more agile animal, say a bobcat, a lean leaping ghost with splayed pads and tight haunches.

The dead girl wanted to try it. Kelly promised to bring her right back.

Greg hesitated. "It looks dangerous to me."

"We take people every day. Amanda be fine."

"Take your camera," her father called after.

Kelly led her around the bend. "You got to climb up this little rise to get there."

Her face went slack. "Are you serious?"

"Grab hold of that laurel, Amanda. That plant there. There you go. Give you a boost."

Kelly gave it—touching her!—and she pulled herself up. Over the rise, she saw the last waterfall. It was nothing more than a tiny gurgling delta. She began to laugh.

She turned around and found Kelly there. He had a dusky look, shards of coal dust imbedded in his face. Nine years in the Haymaker Mine, riding the mantrip into the belly of the mountain. At night, his skin leaked metal. He woke to blue slivers on the pillow. He kissed her open mouth. She felt his beard and its pleasant rasp on her skin. Swallows singing through the air, soft blue sickles. And the two worlds touch, in a way we always hoped they could. Kelly jumped the wall. He became one of them.

"I turned that raft over," Kelly said. "I turned it over on purpose."

"My God," said Reed, "them people trusted you. My God, that's fucking awful, that's *terrible*."

The air crackled with alarm. Kelly stared at the river, the sculpted earth and water.

"'Deed I did. Her dad was looking at us," Kelly said. "He come up behind and saw."

Reed went on mindlessly, "No, no, no."

"I know these falls. Think I'd make a mistake right here? These falls is my bread and butter. Been over a thousand times. Been over them blindfolded."

Everyone yelling, "What'd he see? What was he gone do?" Frenzied and shouting just anything that came to mind.

"I had to. I didn't mean to drown her," Kelly said. "Just her dad."

That settled in. Chet was saying, "Hold on! Kelly, you did it because he seen you and her?"

"She wanted me to get rid of him."

"Wait—"

"She hated her dad. She didn't care if he seen us. He wasn't her kind. He wasn't like us."

We took in his words.

"She told you that?"

"Listen," he said. "Listen to the water."

"What?"

"She told me yesterday," Kelly said.

It started with cursing. You could taste anger in the air, taste it on your tongue. We'd been had. Kelly didn't have two worlds. He had one, ours, the lesser. "You evil liar," Chet Mason told him. Kelly babbled on. Everyone howled at him to quit.

"She told me today."

We shut him up the only way we could. He slid and danced under our hands. Reed had to take off his belt and hit him with the buckle. Grabbing hold of crazy arms and kicking legs, we flung Kelly into that blind, sucking roar. He flopped in with a smack.

Raw white noise. Kelly was gone. Had we really done it? The Gauley took him under. We blinked wildly at one another. No one said a thing. Let it drag him to the ocean.

The river made a shushing sound. We hadn't kept track of the days. Sweet's Falls trickled down to nothing. The Army Corps had lowered its levers. The water was placid. A carnival ride unplugged. Kelly floated to the surface, sputtering, blinking at the sky.

Gauley Season was over. He paddled to the riverbank and pulled himself ashore with fistfuls of cattail. Bloody, he managed a grin and gave us a thumbs-up.

Nothing's painful as embarrassment. Our credulousness stung like bedsores. Even now we nurse those wounds.

Outlandish as it was, Kelly's story nagged at you. There were three witnesses: two dead, the other lost in that white country of madness. Could it be true? Part of you wanted to believe Kelly flipped the raft on purpose. Kelly and the girl—rafters and locals, one people—a beautiful story. That is, a mawkish lie. If Kelly Bischoff can't equal them—to know their names, brush their lips, be loved, respected—no one on Pillow Rock can. Once again, the world let us know what we are. Swallows in flight. The rasp of shoes. Kelly built himself a legend on that. He believed. Maybe he'd come to cherish the girl out of a terrible guilt, which can midwife the strongest, most wretched kind of love into the world. Those cold nights on the Route 19 overpass, he believed. For a man like him, like us, one mistake—one botched run over the falls—could ruin him forever. It wasn't entirely his fault. When they signed the papers, the rafters delivered their lives into Kelly's hand, they bought the thrill of giving yourself over to a stranger, and the bill came due. And we were the ones who chose Kelly, after all, one of ours. We let the girl die. When Chet Mason reached for Kelly's hand, we damned him to his own true life. A life with us. But Kelly couldn't let go of the dream. He couldn't join in our quiet decline.

Soured by it all, we gave Pillow Rock back to the rattlesnakes. Now, we let them lie coiled to soak up the heat like powerful conductors.

We found ways to occupy our time: machining engines, welding catch-gates, jacklighting deer. The lesser waters no one coveted, so we dove off the cliffs at Summersville Lake till the state fenced it off. Then we cut the wire with bolt cutters—the West Virginia credit card—and dove at night, our jacklights trained on green water, attracting a fine mist of moths and mayflies.

Yet Gauley Season never ceased to be part of our year. The rafters buy potato chips and high-test, they flag us down for directions, but they don't miss us, our catcalls from the rock. They palm tips into knowing hands, book next season's trip, tighten luggage racks on foreign cars. As we do our chores, we imagine the shredding water, the cry of clients, the slur of rubber on stone.

They slalom down Sweet's Falls with nothing but the growl of water in their ears. We hate them. We hate them with the fury that is the same as love.

The rafters notice a single man perched on the granite. Shirt-less, Kelly Bischoff raises a hand or touches a hat brim. A wise, gray-bearded fisherman gone down to ply the waters. Hair lank, skin mottled like a Plott hound's. Bedraggled, harried by weather and briar, the river guide has earned this lonesome place by great effort, by true compass. Stalwart, wiry, keen of limb. A true moun-taineer, rifle-true. But they know no better. The river guide has made good on his mortgage. With the yellow tusks of a bulldozer, he breaks the mountain. He draglines the coal.

The river guide cups his hands and calls to the rafters, but they can't hear, they tip over the falls and lose sight of him in a joyous crush.

The nude crag of Pillow Rock, stripped of its people, scrawled and scrimshawed in the shit of swallows. They don't know that we—the true fishermen—will not return until season's end, rods ready, faces hard, when the heavens part, the rotors of helicopters mutter their staccato hymn, and we receive the silver benediction of government fish.

TELEMETRY

O N A GOOD DAY, SURGERY LASTS three minutes or less. Today's takes longer. Kathryn has an audience.

They don't touch the fish at this point—they try to handle them as little as possible—but for the girl, Kathryn makes an exception. She wets her hand in a clear plastic bucket and lifts the stunned fish from the net. A wild brook trout, with a beating heart no bigger than a ruby. The girl leans in to wonder at the gently heaving side, the cool, vermiculated skin. It comes to life and squirms in Kathryn's hand. She grips down—gentle, but firm. The girl squeals a little. She can't be more than seven. She has the kind of light blond hair that darkens with age. In ten years she'll pick up a picture of herself and see a stranger.

"Wet your hand," Kathryn says.

Kathryn has to stop thinking of her as *the girl*. Her name is Shelly. Kathryn's never been able to see children as real people. She wonders what this says about her. Shelly puts a tentative finger to an adipose fin, a sleek belly, a black mouth.

In Kathryn's first summer on Back Allegheny Mountain, the trout and the bright scalpel made her squeamish. Fear of killing something so delicate, so rare. Two years later, the work is rote.

She has to remind herself of the beauty of the place: its rich pelt of red spruce and wildflowers, its pools of glacial blue, each set like a sapphire in the spiky ring of a beaver dam. She doesn't notice the sweet balsam on the wind, or the river smell, equal parts iron and moss. The odd bear will wander through camp and savage a cooler, reminding her of what the mountain still is. The Monongahela National Forest begins a mile downstream. A ski resort owns this land, ten thousand acres. So far, they have left this part undeveloped—or *underdeveloped,* as the Chamber of Commerce says.

"You better toss him in."

A male voice behind them. Gary, bossy as always, is standing knee-deep in the Shavers Fork of the Cheat River. It laps at crudely mended neoprene waders. Lifting the electroshock wand high overhead, he reaches a free hand down to the river. He takes a palmful of water and rubs it over his face. Water droplets gather in a patchy beard, each a prism.

"By the book, by the book," he crows. "What would the University Animal Care and Use Committee say? Ain't you a member of said committee?"

Kathryn rolls her eyes. Shelly smiles at that. Kathryn dumps the trout into another plastic bucket, cold creek water dosed with a clove-oil solution. An anesthetic and antiseptic. Shock, drug, cut. A wonder it doesn't kill them. The trout swims in a lovely sinuous line, resting on nervous fins. Sleek skin the color of mint and coal-fire. The trout lists to its side, loses equilibrium, and floats to the surface. Kathryn scoops it up.

Her scalpel licks its side, below the ventral line. A clean incision, millimeters.

"Give it here."

She takes the telemetry device from Shelly's palm. A mechanized pill, clear and crammed with minute machinery, with a fiber-optic tail. It recalls the sterility of good hospitals, all mankind can accomplish. Kathryn slides it into the incision. Shelly winces.

"Don't worry," Kathryn says. "He can't feel a thing."

"Fish don't hurt?"

"No. Not that. He's just sleepy."

Initially the trout drove her crazy. The movements seemed erratic. Had the telemeters malfunctioned? Did the new cell-phone tower throw them off? Kathryn had ice-pick headaches and spent a lot of time in her sleeping bag. Patterns then emerged. To say the least, this population is mobile. Maybe the highest rates ever recorded in the mountain chain. Besides the odd flutter of anxiety, she is confident in her numbers.

Kathryn whip-stitches three sutures to close the incision and eases the trout into a bucket of plain river water. As they wait for the clove oil to wear off, she explains their research to Shelly, how they track the movement of brook trout between the main stem and the tiny tributaries. How far do they go? Do they migrate because of rising water temperatures? Is there an identifiable trigger?

"If you come back tomorrow, I'll show you how. We use a radio transmitter. It's fun. It's like on TV."

"Thanks for showing me, Kathy."

"Kathryn. It's Kathryn."

She smiles at the girl quickly, ferociously—a bad habit of hers.

Shelly blushes, then runs off in a gawky clatter of limbs. Dumbfounded, Kathryn watches her go. Grasshoppers fling themselves out of her path. One hits the river. A trout snaps it up.

Gary says, "Strike another blow for women in the sciences."

Kathryn laughs, a good sport, though she's disappointed. She wanted to plug a laptop into the generator and show off her program: those dreamy wandering lavender dots, x-axis and y-.

The trout has righted itself. After taking measurements on a digital scale, Kathryn walks it to the water and works it back and forth in the current. Number 30. Gills flare. In a realization she can almost feel, the trout kicks off in a little starburst of relief. The trout's lie is no bigger than a bathtub. She lifts her tickled palm.

Gary wades out and unhitches his pack, dainty for a big man. He respects the equipment. They drive back to camp in her big, bouncing Ford. It parts the field like a frigate. The other member of their team, Michael, the one Kathryn is sleeping with, is still asleep in her tent.

That afternoon, the girl begins stealing. Michael notices first. He finds plastic tubs open, ones they are fastidious about closing. Nothing expensive—a bag of dried apples, a warm bottle of beer. The next day, a flathead screwdriver. At first they think it's the girl's father. They don't know his name. Why not a shotgun, why not the GPS?

And Michael says, "Of course it's the kid. She walks past a thousand-dollar laptop for a bag of cereal."

"Shelly?"

Gary gawps at them. "You've got a double agent on your hands."

They glance over at the only other camp, a good hundred yards off. Muddy blue jeans strung on a line. A resiny ax wedged in a hemlock. The pup tent is bedraggled, decades old. A sharp contrast to the researchers'. Kathryn's truck is solid with gear. Enough to invade a small Arab nation, Michael says. This makes her feel bloated. Those bins packed solid with food, electronics, clothes. A glut of technology. Who needs all this shit?

Ever since the pair showed up three days ago, the researchers have sensed something off. First, a man near thirty and a little girl alone—you assume the worst, no matter how unfair that is. They don't wear hiking boots, but tennis shoes. They don't have a good way to cook their food, just a fire-ring. They are poor. They never came over to say hello—the researchers are desperate for new voices, new faces. Kathryn finally caught the girl watching them and coaxed her over. Her dad has a bruised look around his eyes. At night they hear him talking to himself, or to Shelly, except some nights he does not. He has an army-surplus pack, Korean War vintage.

It's near four when the team makes dinner. They're too disturbed to focus. Gary says, "I'm marching over there and asking them lend of my screwdriver. I need it."

"*Marching over there?*" Michael says. "Leave it alone. They don't have shit."

"I'm pissed. I buy good tools. The best. *Consumer Reports* and everything."

Kathryn says, "Just let it go. Don't be the world's youngest fussy old man."

As soon as she says that, Gary softens, cools, as bland as candle wax. She hates that about him. They spent the first summer here alone, having a grand old time until he drunkenly propositioned her. He was only half joking. She laughed at him. She regrets that. He stalked off to his tent, and they never discussed it. Michael joined in the second year, after his own work fell apart like so much wet cardboard. (He's now exploring the effects of woody debris on trout habitat, a topic Gary calls flimsy, if not to Michael's face.) Michael was studying strip-mining effects on the next watershed over, until he gave a bitter, truthful interview to a newspaper. Consol Coal banned him from its property. Turns out he was sneaking through a hole in the fence, for which he still faces trespassing charges. They have chilling surveillance video of him taking water samples. The department chair bailed Michael out of the Upshur County jail. The chair couldn't have been more proud. He asked—told?—Kathryn to make some room. She invited Michael on before realizing, far too late, that Gary hated him with the dull white fury of an acetylene torch. Both are younger than her, just master's students. Michael is inspired, combative, a sloppy researcher—everything workmanlike Gary is not. Michael is handsome, everyone's favorite. Gary, soft and baggy, is tolerated. Worse, the spite isn't mutual.

Kathryn says, "I'll buy you a new screwdriver."

"Don't patronize me."

"I'll let you chop onions," she says with her sweetest smile.

"The woman said."

"Fuck you."

She says it with cheer. Since the president of Harvard made his comments, they have been paying ironic tribute to Kathryn's role as "woman scientist." Michael fixes on them the cockeyed, pedantic look of a deranged professor. He says, "Domesticity suggests peace. All sociology tells us so. It is the realm of the calmer emotions."

Michael seems more charming than he actually is, when she grits down and listens to what he says. She wonders if this is a tic of evolution—that easy, flashing smile, meant to attract her, distract her, like aluminum foil to a crow. The easing of standards.

Cooking does calm them. Michael leaves to filter water. Gary handles knives. Kathryn primes the portable stove and cups a lit match against the wind, bearing it like an acolyte.

She didn't plan on sleeping with Michael, not up here, not ever. A way to pass the time, she notes glumly. He lives with a girlfriend in Morgantown, a nice third-grade teacher with a flapper haircut, prettier than her. *But who isn't nice?* Kathryn wonders. We're all nice. *Nice, nice, nice.* He's six or seven years younger than Kathryn—that's what stings. It feels so cheap, so glitter-and-trash. She should feel worse about the girlfriend.

Across the field, the man dumps armfuls of branches into the fire-ring, then pours kerosene on them. Their dinner will consist of cans. Maybe they have nowhere else to go.

Shelly steps out of the tent. She's been sleeping. She waves at Kathryn. Kathryn doesn't know what to do, except wave back. The man does too.

"All hail the good thief," Gary says as he whets the knife.

After dinner, Gary scours their pots with sand. When he gets back, he says, "I want to shoot some guns."

"I'm not in the mood," Kathryn says.

"I'm in the mood."

"It's okay," Michael says to Kathryn. "You don't want to bother them, do you?"

"I don't like kids and guns in the same space."

"I'll go talk to them. I'll ask if it's okay."

Gary says, "I don't give a damn. I hauled three gross clay pigeons up here and we are going to shoot every one. We are going to drink beer and we are going to shoot guns. It's Friday night and we are Americans."

"Easy. Five minutes."

As Michael crosses the field, Kathryn packs away the stove. Gary goes round to the far side of the truck, where she can't see him, and sifts through boxes. He slides a double-barreled twelve-gauge out of a soft case and cracks it open. The metal sounds crisp.

It's a safe place to shoot. They camp in "the field," the timber ghost town of Spruce. Nothing's left but scorched foundations, a lone switchman's shack, and the odd pile of rusted peavey-heads in the weeds. At four thousand feet, Spruce was once the highest incorporated town in the east. Fifteen hundred people lived up here—with hotel, church, and post office—but they never buried anyone, the true measure of settlement. Spruce lasted twelve years. It's an old story, no secret place. In spring and fall, fishermen bound for Shavers walk seven miles up the ruined track. Kathryn has finagled a gate key to the private road—she's the only native in the department and knows how to talk—and fishermen are amazed to find a big, dual-wheeled truck parked up there. "How'd you get on that road?" they ask, salivating. "Connections," she says. In bright summer, trout grow wary, and fishermen leave. The researchers have it to themselves. Until that man and his girl appeared.

Birds shatter from the field.

He shot me.

He didn't, no, he shot a beer bottle on a stump. Battering off the ridge, echoes recede in waves. Gary pops open the breech, and twin trails of gun smoke drift. Kathryn has to sit. She pats herself down. She clutches her head, as if to keep it from being unscrewed.

"Sorry! Kathryn, look at me. I didn't mean to scare you. I thought you saw me. I did."

Michael returns with man and daughter in tow. "Hi!" Shelly says to Kathryn.

The man sticks out his hand. "I'm Russ," he says, "Russ Nedermeyer. Good meeting you."

Names and bottles of beer are introduced all around. Nedermeyer keeps on talking. He has an Eisenhower jacket, a brown crewcut under a ball cap, and a five-day beard—in an odd way, he looks clean-shaven just the same. It's his stride, crisp and confident, and he wears a camouflage t-shirt, the kind sporting-goods stores sell from a cardboard box. It sags over a slight belly and blue jeans gone white and soft. Kathryn can tell he's local. He has that accent, somewhere between a twang and a brogue, a run-on voice with words tripping over each other and along. Not southern, but musical and watery, like stones knocking underwater. An accent Kathryn has taken pains to cull from her own throat. She wants to be taken seriously.

Gary says, "You all are on vacation up here."

It's not a question.

Nedermeyer grins. "That's right. Shelly and me are having a big time."

"You like to shoot?"

"Love it."

Everyone makes sure to keep Shelly back, and she revels in the attention. They sink each leg of the clay-pigeon thrower and point it at the forest. The string has dry-rotted, so Gary's bootlace is volunteered. Discs are flung in wild, wobbling arcs, slivers of toxic orange against the blue. They shoot for an hour. Shoulders purple and ache sweetly. Nedermeyer cancels one and cancels the other. He can't miss. He knocks double after double from the sky, the best shot by far.

"I was a piss-poor shot till the navy. You be surprised how much the navy makes you shoot. You wouldn't think that, would you? Maybe we ought to bet money on this. No?"

Between shots, he delivers a running monologue on their family life. Some of it makes Kathryn blush, with Shelly there listening. "Her mom's on drugs. She's living in Baltimore, it's a damned crack house, she don't even get visitation. Wish I was lying to you."

That's hard, they all agree.

Nedermeyer makes a little shrugging hitch with his shoulders. "Her decision. Last time I went, there had to be eight guys in there, smoking the pinkest biker rock you ever seen. Air tasted like Drano on the back of your tongue. Don't marry young, is all I can say. I got Shelly out of there. Judge drug his feet on it like you wouldn't believe. No telling what she saw."

Separately, the adults imagine the vile things Shelly encountered.

Readjusting to this, Kathryn looks at the girl. No response. Shelly's heard all this before. Yellow piles of shotgun hulls accrue at their feet, and Shelly makes a game of racing forward between shots and gathering them up. Nedermeyer hands the shotgun over to Kathryn.

"Knock them down," he says. "Shelly! Get back from there! Throw-arm on that thing'll break your effing leg."

Kathryn shoots a dozen times, missing all but three. She's distracted.

"You lost your touch," Michael tells her.

"It comes and goes." She hands the shotgun back.

Nedermeyer guesses, correctly, that Kathryn grew up shooting. "I can tell."

Gary drinks beer and makes small talk with the girl. He's good with children. It's surprising. Kathryn feels a little off balance. Maybe she's drinking hers too fast.

Nedermeyer tells them, "God, I love this. Been too long. Too long. We used to hunt grouse. Raised English setters. My dad, I mean. No more birds to speak of. Pull!"

Kathryn smiles in spite of herself. Nedermeyer is half the people she went to high school with: a garrulous semi–con man, damn good with tools, maybe a little into drugs, basically harmless. A serious talker. He's a new type for the others. They spent their years in the labs and classrooms of a tamed college town. They don't know the local animals. Gary's from the suburbs of Minneapolis, and Michael grew up in DC, the only white kid in his school.

It's inevitable, so Kathryn asks Nedermeyer where he's from.

They grew up a few miles apart, in Tuscarora County, to the north.

"What's your last name?"

"Tennant," she says.

"Aw, shit. I know your dad." Then, more softly: "Well, I knew him."

Kathryn's heart thrills and saddens at the same time. Nedermeyer doesn't say anything else. He senses not to. She sees that in his face. He offers the box of shells. She waves it off.

Gunpowder curling in her nose. It reminds her of squirrel hunting with her father. No one thought it strange, he had no sons. Her mother would boil two eggs in the dark kitchen, and Kathryn would stick her hands in the pockets of the oversized hunting vest and clutch them for warmth. Once they cooled, she peeled each egg in the woods for a late breakfast. Her father smiled as she popped each yolk, a miniature sun, into her mouth. Before each shot he'd whisper, *Plug your ears.* Sitting on a log with him, she could feel the dull, muffled percussion through her seat, her spine. Bodies fell from the trees. Gathering them into the game bag in her vest. Feeling them lose warmth against her back. Soothing, and strange.

Nedermeyer closes the shotgun with a muted thunk. "Nice piece," he says to Gary. "I like this gun. I like a twenty-six-inch barrel. Nice and quick. Whippy. A bird gun. It's choked improved cylinder and modified? Classic. No sense changing it." He makes a show of looking at the barrel, reading embossed letters. "I never heard of Ithaca before. That a new make?"

"No. The Japanese make it."

Nedermeyer slaps his head and makes a goggle-eyed funny face. His daughter laughs. Kathryn suddenly loves the man.

He looks around. "The mountains," he says. "I love it up here. Even in July. Couldn't live nowhere else. I'm done moving. When I was in the service, it's all I thought of."

They take in the ridgeline, the blue dusk. In the distance, far above the stands of red spruce, the best in the state, the cell tower lights. This is the signal, night is here, time for sweaters. The temperature can drop forty degrees when the sun goes down. Time for tin-punch constellations, and busy satellites tearing arcs in the sky. Even with the resort and the tower, this is the clearest night you can hope for east of the Mississippi, as close as you get to that ancient blackness.

Gary says, "Tell Kathryn that. She's moving."

"Moving? Where to?"

"I'm not sure. I was offered a position. At Arizona State."

Nedermeyer whistles.

"That's what I thought," she tells him.

"What your folks say?"

"Good question." She visited Tempe for a week, taught a class, presented her fisheries research. They loved her—in the swelter, the flatness. Concrete sprawl nibbling at desert, air-conditioning blasting you with its chemical bite. Everyone looking unhealthy and heat stunned and bleached. She could always come back east in the summer, stay with her mom. She tells herself this as if it solves everything. She doesn't answer Nedermeyer's question.

Gary's half-drunk. He says, "You folks hungry? We're making dinner."

Michael and Kathryn look at him with curiosity, but he just grins back. So they make a second dinner, and the five of them eat together, filling out the portable table for the first time.

They begin sharing meals each night, but Shelly keeps on stealing. She and her father stay on for a week, then two. At first they share token supplies with the researchers—a sliced loaf of store-bread, peanut butter—till they run out of food. No one mentions it. Stranger things disappear: a battered water bottle, a bottle opener, a new jug of bleach for sterilizing materials. Nothing expensive: fly rods, the Bushnell rangefinder, and laptops stay put. It feels more like a game than a violation. A magpie of a girl. It doesn't matter. In a week, Kathryn will make the thirty-mile trip to Elkins for supplies.

At this point, her research demands no more than two or three hours a day, so she spends time with Shelly—maybe she's stealing out of boredom. Kathryn takes her swimming in the afternoons, something they both love. The others stay behind to play cutthroat euchre.

Kathryn lends her a towel, and they walk to the flat rock by a ruined trestle. The Shavers Fork of the Cheat is a shallow river, and even out in the channel, the water comes only to Kathryn's breastbone. They bring biodegradable soap. They step over a pile of broken crawdads where coons made a meal. The sun is glorious. Mica glitters in the rock.

Kathryn feels hesitation—taking off her clothes with someone else's child—but in a moment, they're naked. She can't imagine doing this in any other context. Shelly's body is just becoming girlish, winnowing itself out of a child's frame, but naked, she still has a child's lack of self-consciousness. She doesn't know to be ashamed. At seven? Kathryn worries for that, wondering if it has to do with how Shelly was raised. For her part, Shelly gazes full on at Kathryn, a grown woman, unabashed. Esteeming her, the loose breasts, the trim nest of hair. Kathryn doesn't mind, children are curious, but when they're in the water, she takes care not to touch the girl, not to graze a swimming leg. The rock is pleasant and hot. She loves being naked in the sun. If Gary would leave. Maybe he'll volunteer for Elkins. She tries not to think of sex. She hopes Michael doesn't ask about her father.

They ease in over rounded, mossy stones and find the water pleasantly cool, a touch under sixty. Shadows dart to the edge of the pool. Kathryn soaps herself, then hands it over. She wonders if Shelly would have washed otherwise. If Nedermeyer would have cared.

Shelly puts her hand to the current and carves out a white plume of water.

Kathryn closes her eyes for a moment—just a moment—and sinks under. Back at camp, surely, over cards, Nedermeyer is telling them about her father. It can't be helped. It nettles just the same. Hell, Nedermeyer is probably related to someone at Green Valley Mine—probably related to *her*. No more than ten thousand people in Tuscarora County. When Kathryn was an undergraduate, her father died in the mines. Everyone knows how the miners were trapped behind a coal rib for eleven hours, before the expired rescue masks failed and methane saturated their lungs. Her mom: *You have to come home, you have to come home*. Kathryn remembers the phone call. At ten in the morning, she was still in bed, groggy from a party, hungover. She still feels guilty, it's the one thing that can make her throat burn, make her cry. Kathryn borrowed a roommate's car and drove half-drunk, the windows down. She arrived in the clothes she'd slept in, smelling of stale beer. The mine under a siege of news trucks. Shouts. The ragged sound of weeping. Parked cars lining the highway.

In the last minutes, her father scrawled a note in huge, amoebic letters: *Don't worry for us. We're not hurting. It's just like falling asleep. I love you all and I will see you in the next world. I will wait on you*. Now her mother lives in that grim pillbox of a house, where her father's hats are lined up neatly on pegs, his work boots nocked in a stand by the door.

A computer says her new office would be 2,100.6 miles from where she sleeps on this mountain. Her mother's house, 43.1. She can leave all this behind. In one swipe of the ax.

Shelly snaps her awake with an awful, gut-shot howl. *Oh God, she's drowning*.

Kathryn claws wet hair from her eyes. A snake shatters the water, a bolt of silver in its mouth. Then Shelly laughs at herself, and Kathryn does, too. It races off.

"He ate your fish!"

"That's okay. We'll track him, too."

Thirty fish tagged per summer. They make adjustments for mortality. A crass statement: "Adjustments for mortality." Science and its flat, brutal affect.

They climb onto the rock and dry themselves. Kathryn asks for the soap.

"I think I lost it."

It's hidden, of course, under Shelly's folded clothes. Kathryn feels ill, and feels like she would never want a child of her own: the winsome liars. After a long grating pause, she says, "Shelly, if you need anything from me, you just ask, okay? Just ask me. If you want to have lunch or go swimming or get a ride back to town. No games, okay? Don't be shy."

Shelly says okay. Her voice is hollow.

"You don't have to take things."

Kathryn can feel it on her skin. That stinging blush. They are being watched.

"Get dressed. Quick. Someone's coming."

They drag on clothes. They listen. They stare at the laurel hell on the far bank. Nothing.

Kathryn tells herself it was a bear, a bobcat, a doe.

When they get back to the field, Michael has the stove primed, and Gary's setting out plates. Nedermeyer isn't around. Was he watching them?

He steps out of his tent palming a huge Vidalia onion he forgot he had.

They make omelets for dinner. Nedermeyer laughs at that, but they need to use the last of their eggs. Red peppers, green peppers, yolk yellow—all the colors of life.

He asks, "How you all paying for this operation?"

Gary—because he wrote the application—brags on the funds they're receiving from the Fish and Wildlife Service, plus a grant from Mead-WestVaCo, a paper conglomerate trying to clean up its image. Trout Unlimited wants to "rebuild" the river, a multimillion-dollar project. A hundred years ago, companies dynamited the boulders and channels to turn the main stem into one big flume. The only deep pools left are a dozen places where railroad trestles cross the river, totally manmade. The winterkill is staggering.

"The pricks," says Nedermeyer. "We just bent over and let them do it. Begged them to."

"The river can come back," Gary promises.

Kathryn disagrees. Downstream of here, the resort sloughs too much sediment into the water. It smothers fish eggs in the nest, even in minimal amounts. The only thing that could fix this place is another orogeny, new mountains, glaciation—a cataclysm. But she says nothing.

Nedermeyer croons, "Just give it time, give it time. And this one here wants to leave!"

He winks at Kathryn. Her eyes go glassy with embarrassment.

Michael flips an omelet expertly. When it's slightly brown, he takes a fork and tips it turtle onto Shelly's plate. She reaches for the catsup and sets out, as Michael says, to ruin a perfectly good omelet. She puts back the catsup. He says, "I was just teasing. Take it."

Nedermeyer asks, "How much river you working?"

"Spruce down to First Fork."

"Super-interesting. I run radar in the navy. Nuclear subs."

"Did you?"

They readjust their feelings toward him. He laughs that musical laugh of his.

"I'd love to see what you do. Shelly says you hurt them, but you're awful nice about it."

They decide to tag a fish for the hell of it tomorrow and show off their gear. After dinner, Nedermeyer says, "This is a whole lot of fun. I wish we could pay you back. Me and Shelly appreciate this."

Gary says, "You'll figure something out."

•

After inserting the telemeter, Michael slips a dazed nine-inch brook trout into the water. A slash of bronze takes the poor thing and disappears.

"Jesus! Looked like a fucking water spaniel. About took your hand off, didn't he?"

"Get me the pack," Michael says.

A German brown trout so big the electric shock doesn't even stun it, just sends it jumping and shirking and headshaking, dousing them all. Kathryn leaps on it with both hands. When she lifts the thrashing hook-jawed brown, it disgorges the bedraggled brook trout they just tagged. Michael saves the telemeter, slitting open the sutures. With a digital camera, they take hero shots gripping the fish—a grand female with scarred, scored flanks—and measure her. Over eight pounds, with a girth of fifteen inches. Statistically speaking, a larger fish than this river can support. Like finding a battleship in a parking garage. After wrecking the native trout population, the timber outfits introduced the fast-growing hatchery browns, and they've been here since, in token numbers. Cannibals. They promise to mail Shelly a copy of her picture.

"That's the fish of a lifetime," Nedermeyer says. "A guy'd kill for that. You see a lot like this?"

Gary says, "No. Not at all. We've caught some nudging twenty-four inches under the trestles, but nothing like this. Can you imagine her in the fall? She'd carry three pounds of eggs."

Nedermeyer drinks from a battered water bottle, one taken from the researchers' camp. He doesn't bother hiding it. Maybe Shelly told him it was a gift. He hands it to Michael, who takes a drink and says, "Let's track this one, too. For the hell of it."

"We don't do invasive species," Kathryn says.

Gary cries, "Listen to the hissing of the sacred geese! Come on. It's a salmonid. I'm just curious. Please. Don't kill my joy. I'm an invasive species myself, of Eurocentric origin. Let us deduce the secrets of the dirty German fish."

"Absolutely not. It'll throw off my numbers."

Michael lifts the trout, not quite as gingerly as he would a delicate native, to show off its leopard-spotted sides—cracked peppercorns, sunbursts of red, coronas of blue. The underbelly like rich, burnt butter. *Brown*: such a miserly name. The Linnaean, *Salmo trutta*, is so much to be preferred. And the melodic freshwater morpha: *fario, lacustris.*

Nedermeyer asks, "You mind if I fish around here?"

The gleaming eyes of an excited fisherman. *Here we go*, Kathryn tells herself. He's seen the unused fly rods Gary and Michael brought to the mountain. Like all men in coldwater fisheries, they grew up loving to fish. After a year in the program, they're sick of it. In three summers, Gary has fished all of twice. The electroshock wand makes fishing silly. It drains the river of mystery, of secrets, when you know what lives there. But even Gary and Michael are giddy now.

Kathryn says coolly to Nedermeyer, "I didn't know you came here to fish."

"I didn't know this river had big-ass trout in it. Damn."

Michael and Kathryn exchange looks. "Well," she says, "we can't stop you. I mean, we're using these fish to do *research*. I wouldn't want you frying up a mess of our test subjects."

"I'll throw big streamers for big fish. Not your itty-bitty ones. Can I borrow your rod?"

The odds of catching the big female are slim, especially in the clear, skinny water of July. Kathryn knows they'll never see the trout again. Let him have his pointless fun.

And why did she go into the field? A twinge of pleasure, of knowledge. Her dad would pull over to the side of a bridge, and they would watch from above, before he slipped down the bank to catch them. She was charmed by the motions of trout. How they take their forms from the pressures of another world, the cold forge of water. Their drift, their mystery, the way they turn and let the current take them, take them, with passive grace. They turn again, tumbling like leaves, then straighten with mouths pointing upstream, to better sip a mayfly, to root up nymphs, to watch for the flash of the heron's bill. The current always trues them, like compass needles. When she watches them, she feels wise.

Michael slips the trout back into the water. Gills rustle, blood-rich. The fins toggle.

"Fuck it," Kathryn says. "Why not? Oh. Sorry, Shelly."

"For what?"

Two days later, when Nedermeyer manages to catch that massive trout, they have a late Fourth of July party in celebration. It's enough to feed the five of them, if not fill them. Kathryn sulks a little—not that she's anti-fishing, she just didn't want to see it killed—till Gary reminds her it's an invasive species, a trashy European fish that pops her precious native brook trout like potato chips. A massacre artist! The Ted Bundy of fish! In the scheme of things, a minor sin. She decides to get kind of drunk and let live. They couldn't believe it when Nedermeyer carried the trout into camp. It was long as a lady's stocking. Shelly danced about it, clapping hands.

"What can I say? I got good luck."

After scaling it, Nedermeyer fills the body cavity with sweet onions and a strip of bacon. He wraps the trout in tinfoil and cooks it over the fire on a blackened grillwork. He disdains their portable stove. With raw fire, he bakes potatoes and cinnamon apples and roasts field corn, showing Shelly how to blacken each ear just so. For all his roughness, he's a good, doting father. Kathryn fleetingly pictures having a child with him—a thought that dances through her brain like a feather on the wind. The trout's flesh is pink and flaky like a salmon's and falls apart. It has been eating crawdads, and the beta-carotene gives the flesh highlights of reddish richness. With the tines of a fork, Nedermeyer lifts out a delicious cheek and pops it into Shelly's mouth.

It's been a decade, at least, since any of the researchers have eaten trout.

Afterward, they fire off leftover Roman candles, taking care to stomp out loose fires that flare in the grass. Balls of light skitter and douse themselves in the river. Gary pulls out his gas-station harmonica and plays the four songs he knows. The wind begins to blow.

A clean linen moon rises over the mountain's worn crest. Swaying a bit, Michael leaves to piss and wash his hands at the river. He's gone a long time. The music manages to be rude, brassy, and sweet. They hear Michael out in the weeds. The world is raucous with tree frogs.

On a night like this, with music and chill summer air, Kathryn loves West Virginia. There are places on the map called Tennant Run, and a Tennant Cemetery in a hollow back of Circleville. Tuscarora County, where people are old-time Republicans and German stock, like her mother, a Propst. The boulderfields, the spaces empty of people—a lonesomeness city-dwellers could never comprehend. Sometimes it seems you know animals more intimately than people. Beaver heads cutting wake in the water, bear shit jeweled with seeds, deer quenching themselves in the river's cool. Her family has lived here for three hundred years. But the place is wretchedly poor and backward and may never be right. She's thirty-one, unmarried and maybe doesn't want to be, with a little tuck in her smile. In a way, Nedermeyer is more correct for her—at least, that's what her home tells her she deserves. Her relatives call her one of those *professional students*, with a touch of teasing, a touch of scorn, a frost-core of jealousy. Even her mother. *You got any men following you around? No? I can't believe that.*

Michael returns, carrying an empty jug he found in the weeds. Clorox. He throws it and hits Nedermeyer square in the chest. In a second, they are standing face to face.

"You dumped bleach in the river. Under the railroad trestle. Come on!"

"Hold on now, I caught that fish, you saw me."

"I didn't see shit! You killed that fish with bleach."

"Shelly saw."

Don't look at her, Kathryn tells herself. This is happening too fast. Everyone knows this county has a grand tradition of fishing with bleach, quarter sticks of dynamite, bottles of carbide.

"There's probably more dead ones. Probably ours."

"Oh my God," Kathryn says.

Nedermeyer begins to blush, and it's hard to tell if it's from anger or embarrassment. "I caught it legal. I been fishing all my life. It's no trick."

"A gallon of bleach. Do you have any idea how bad this is?"

Shelly has her hands over her ears. She's crying.

"You can't prove that."

Gary smirks and Nedermeyer tells him, "Shut your mouth, fat ass."

Michael lights into him. He calls him a redneck, calls him nine types of motherfucker. "People like you have ruined this place," he says. "Ruined it."

In a book or a movie, this would be the hinge of Shelly's life. The public shaming. Lightheaded now, Kathryn tries to remember a time like this with her dad. All she can recall is a day they went fishing the Elk, and when they returned, a redheaded man with a crooked jaw was leaning against their truck. *Thought he was my buddy's. I was fixing to leave a note.* He left, walking fast. They found scratches on the paint where he'd tried to pry open the lock with a penknife. Her dad said, *Well, you just never know what to expect from people.*

Nedermeyer says, "You finished your speech? You're awful proud of it." He looks to Kathryn and asks her, "Can't you talk some sense into these people?"

She realizes this was supposed to happen, that she would be called upon. When nothing comes, he cries out, "I knew your dad!"

She doesn't know what to say.

"Come on," Nedermeyer says to his daughter. "I'm not about to expose you to this kind of shit."

Nedermeyer takes her by the hand. Crossing the field, they leave the researchers to the ruins of their party, to a sudden nip on the wind. Rain. When it comes, the researchers listen to it hissing in the fire.

No one wants to be first to slink off to the tents. They stand in silence, till a cracking summer downpour drives them inside, after three weeks of dry, to listen to the wet and deafening roar.

The sun comes up white and indistinct, shining through a gauze of humid sky. The researchers drift from sleep at the same time into a sodden camp. Across the field, the rain-crushed tent shines in the sun. The man and the girl must be miserable.

Then they realize the tent has been abandoned, and the doors of Kathryn's truck are hanging open.

What they see stuns them.

Their clothes scattered across the field like dead men. The shotgun buried to its chamber in the mud. Their logbooks heavy with rain. A lantern smashed like a melon on a rock. Their laptops flung in the river. Their research wrecked. Nedermeyer and his daughter long gone.

The researchers are numb. Michael says they should take an inventory, so they unload the truck, reckoning up the damage. With a quizzical look, Michael holds up an unopened jug of bleach he finds in the back. The one they thought Shelly stole. He found it under the seat.

By the dead fire, Gary picks up the Clorox from the night before and examines it.

"Oh no."

"What?"

He tips it over and shows them 06/1995 embossed on the bottom. "It was trash," he says in a small voice. "It wasn't his. It's been here forever."

Back at the state university, the people at computing manage, somehow, to salvage the hard drive from one of the laptops. A minor miracle. Their summer, Kathryn tells everyone, is saved. Then she regrets telling anyone about it at all.

Her paper shows that brook trout, *Salvelinus fontinalis*, in the Shavers Fork of the Cheat River, travel an incredible amount—as far as fifty meters a day, and nearly six kilometers up- and downriver—though the ones residing in tributaries keep still, more or less.

Everyone calls it a very fine piece of work. She presents at conferences around North America. The people at Arizona State send her congratulatory notes.

But on that awful morning on the mountain, the project was doomed. Kathryn sprawled on the flat rock, sluggish with guilt and dew-heavy clothes, believing death to be easier than life. In the grand scheme, did it matter? A fish no longer than a salad fork, and botched research, and what a girl thinks of her father. Small things, really. The small geography of their lives.

But it would set her back a year, she thought, another year lost when she felt, rightly or wrongly, that she didn't have many to spare. Kathryn felt sun on her wrists, her neck. She hadn't felt this way since she saw the spidery blue tipple and knew her father was dying underfoot, somewhere, somehow, in that hug of stone. Was she standing on him? Drills, ambulances, mine executives giving their press conference—they meant nothing.

The private road was too muddy to drive on without tearing it up. That was the worst. The researchers had to wait another day to leave the mountain. Again the clouds rolled in.

Rain smacking nylon, the only sound in the world, and not a smudge of light, not even from the tower. Michael didn't come to Kathryn's tent that night. She was disappointed. She hoped he would, so she could turn him back. She had decided to leave this place for good.

THE ISLAND IN THE GORGE OF THE GREAT RIVER

IN SEPTEMBER OF 1890, THE COUNTY sent the dying to the island. This scrap of ground, ten or twelve acres, would have been unremarkable if not for the fact that it was surrounded by water. The island was in the gorge of a brute river, the New, so unruly that the coal had to be hauled out by rail. The track had taken four years to lay, including tunnels.

There was talk—courthouse talk—of stringing a cable ferry to send the dying across, but in the end, rafts and pirogues were made to do. To build any bridge from the mainland would be foolish—what if a heedless patient ran it back some night and brought society his disease?

Late in the evening, to arouse as little notice as possible, the New River boatmen tied bandannas about their own mouths, all the way up to the eyes, and took pains not to inhale too much, despite their rowing, despite the shortness of their breath. They wouldn't look at the dying people who reclined in their boats. Drawing close, they heard the puttering of a weird machine: the steam autoclave into which the doctor stuffed bandages. Afterward, their hard money won, the boatmen washed down their hands and implements with burning lye.

●

The island had been timbered over like the rest of the lands, so from the far shore you could see the dying who milled about. It was just far enough out in the river to render the people a blurry mystery—this near the mouth of Pinch Creek, where it spilled coal slurry into the New. A tote road gave way to a muddy landing where boatmen had tramped down the bank.

Across the water, the dying and their nurses slid from building to building, digging graves, washing laundry, unhooking themselves from voluminous greenbrier, wincing in the powerful sun. Not that anyone on the mainland stared. That would have been in poor taste. And the region was thinly populated anyhow. The nearest settlement was the coal camp of Pinch, four miles up-hollow, and the miners of Pinch never left. Few people had call to pass by the island.

Except for the roaming gang of boys. They wished they had field glasses to look through, or even a tube of parchment paper. They left the landing to get a better view, finding the fisherman's trail that ran for miles along the river, a mere ditch through weeds and the rank, green smell of life. They waved to the islanders. Now and again, an islander waved back.

"I know that one," said a loud boy named Burl.

"Oh no, you don't," the others said. To deny him this glamour.

"Yeah I do. Look."

This islander was a girl their age, nine, ten.

She lifted her skirt and shrieked, a joyful sound that cut through the whitewater roar. The boys couldn't see much, but the pale flash struck them. She wore nothing beneath. At first they were shocked, then fell to the ground in laughing piles. She turned around and let the skirt drop.

The boys would remember it all their lives—or John Drew would, anyhow. He felt things more than most. The greatest day.

MATTHEW NEILL NULL

John Drew, sheepish, turned away. He couldn't believe what he saw.

The girl ran off to the infirmary building. There were two or three other dying on the far shore, but none paid the girl's antics any mind, absorbed as they were in the end of time.

"John Drew loves a dead girl," Burl chanted. "John Drew loves a dead girl." They laughed at blushing John Drew. They skipped stones, seeing if they could make it to the wretched island.

For days John Drew thought of that girl across the waters. She lifted her skirt at him, only him. He was sure of that.

He returned to Pinch, waiting for the mine whistle to break the day into pieces. When it did, the miners surfaced with empty lunch buckets, leaving the portal, walking the narrow main drag with its bank, post office, and commissary. They found their own company shacks in straggling rows three deep, each one identical, with the same stovepipe, same curl of smoke, same yellow dog lazing in a bare yard, its tail beginning to wag. John Drew's father returned in the fall of evening, shedding bituminous dust. The home a dingy white blur in front of him, eyes still adjusting. The family came out to greet him. He patted John Drew on the back. Behind the shacks, beehive coke ovens in the hillside pulsed redly in the night.

John Drew's father bathed on the porch in a galvanized tub, his nails forever lined in black, the chunk of lye a rock in his fist. An oil lamp stood on a ladder-back chair. Its light drew stoneflies off the river, pert yellow sallies and bigger black ones with orange collars that looked clerical. John Drew walked out to pass time with his father, as he would. Their schedules hardly crossed, save for Sundays, taken up with church. Cooking smells from other shacks came to them. John Drew lived for these moments.

"I went to see them sick people."

His father winced. The man had a long-handled brush in hand and could strike you with it. He was broad across the chest, solid as a keg of nails.

"No," John Drew corrected, "I just looked acrost. I didn't go."

His father knowingly scraped arms with soap, the water turning to silt. "I feel bad for them people. I do. But the county's damned foolish. People use that water. My God, them nurses washing and burning rags and burying, and just hells of people downriver." His father's voice was dreamy.

"That won't hurt us."

"Listen! That river goes right to Fayetteville. That's the county seat. Won't be nobody fit to work. They'll shut down the mines. I'm just waiting on the day I see that yellow flag flying."

John Drew felt the twisting pain—his father had grabbed him hard by the suspenders, not hatefully, but enough to startle and hurt him. Bathwater sloshed all over his clothes.

"I don't want you swimming. Stay up here. I don't want you fishing neither. Who was with you? Who?"

John Drew couldn't lie. "Burl and them others."

"Who?"

"Jaimy. Ow. Buddy."

"That woman lets Burl run wild. John, I hate this damned county government. Them people in Fayetteville just do what they wish. If I see that damned commissioner, I'll give him five knots."

His father let go. John Drew stood there, breathing hard.

In afternoons, after school, overcome by his day of longing, John Drew would walk the great river, before the sun went down, alone these times.

He never spoke to the girl—the river was too much for young voices. They would wave back and forth, she would smile, but she never lifted her skirt like before.

Then, one day, she tossed a thing in the water: a bottle! He ran through briars that ripped his shirt and waded out on the shoal. He reached for the bottle and missed. It was out too far in the curl of the current. The New, of course, swept it on, around the bend. Where did it go? Maybe on to other rivers, maybe as far as Baltimore City, to the ocean and milldams. John Drew could die. He would mourn the bottle's lost message all his life—surely a paper note was corked inside, though there was no way of telling, really. He kicked the water. When his mother saw his shirt, she pitched a fit. He didn't care a pin.

In October, the girl quit arriving to their afternoons. No one moved on the island much. The dying had repaired to the infirmary, to rest in cots, be fanned by nurses, prepare for the end that was rushing them down. John Drew waited for a week, then two. He had piercing headaches—the form his shock took.

Burials took place of a morning, so John Drew never witnessed them. Of a night, when he was home in his family's shack, boatmen brought a few more sick to replace the dead. He had no idea how they came and went. She could be dead. Or she could be shunning him. He wasn't sure which was worse.

The only person still moving on the island was a bearded man who split wood with a short-handled maul. When he noticed John Drew, he walked to the river's edge, cupped his hands, and bellowed to go on now. Go. John Drew stood awhile, to show he didn't care. Water stood between them. John Drew no longer had friends. He had this place, and this girl—the sinew of his days, now stripped out and gone for good. He accepted the fact with grim resolve, as his father had taught him. Once, it seemed so long ago, a dog of theirs had vanished, a mountain cur, and they found it dead upon the ridge in a cold season—some predator had worried it apart. Ice had formed in thin crystals in the red, ripped cave of its belly. Could your own true blood freeze? The ribs stood. He didn't cry. His father was watching him watch the dog. He didn't cry.

Going back to the river was different, though. He couldn't stop himself from that.

Then, only then, John Drew sees her again. The girl is flying a kite. It cracks in the wind, so angular, so white, made of stolen sheets. She twists the string and makes it buck-dance and wheel. John Drew follows the kite with his gaze—he has never seen a thing so pretty. She walks it up and down the bank like a tethered calf, thinly smiling, her admirer following as she drifts it to the island's point. The string breaks. The kite crosses the river and falls at John Drew's feet. Well, not at his feet, but near enough in the laurel he knows it's meant for him.

The struts are broken, but he takes the sheet in hand, holds it close, wraps it round his fist, touching what she'd touched. He will mend the struts with green branches and gut and mail it back across. He'll tie a note to the tail. Sure, she can read—he imagines her quite intelligent. He lifts the fabric to his lips. He waves goodbye, a gesture she returns with a hand slender as a lancet in the distance, and he is lanced by all he feels. Too far away to notice how wan she is, how she musters the dregs of strength to go outside and parade her weeping boils.

The kite is carried home.

It doesn't take long to fix a kite. It doesn't take long for his brother and sister to fall ill. It doesn't take long for his mother to go to bed in despair. Thinking nothing of it, shortly after John Drew brings it home, she finds the sheet and cuts it up for kitchen rags. She scrubs plates, table, sill. Fastidiously she distributes the disease. Boils break on his brother and sister. Tethered boats rock on the river.

John Drew says nothing. He's disappointed when he finds the

sheet is gone, but he scrounges up a gingham cloth, to give the kite something to fly upon.

His parents hide the children in back of the house and quit talking to neighbors, quit all but the mines, even quit the church, a scandal. Their mother is glassy-eyed, silent. When will the neighbors realize? How long before the county sends the children away? This is hell. This is a father's hell.

Frantic, not angry, not even sound of mind, cajoling. "You didn't swim acrost, did you?"

John Drew can't speak.

"I know. I'm sorry," his father says, taking John Drew's arm in a soft grip. "You're a good fine fellow." His father is near to weeping, and he looks a different man altogether. An empty keg. A hollowed skin. "You always been."

He's supposed to respect his father, honor a good name, but at this talk, this soft grip, this begging, John Drew feels disgust wash over him. Can the father sense it? John Drew's father is looking him in the eye, plumbing this stranger who shares his blood, but he's too addled to learn anything of worth. A decade later, he will see John Drew outside a poolroom in the state capital and say, after a moment of hesitation, "Son, why didn't you come home? There's nothing so bad you can't come home." John Drew won't know what to say. What has he been doing all these years? Working, it seems: his clothes, there in Ruffner Avenue, will smell of singed hair and tannery putrefaction. He'll drop his cigarette, shy of the habit. The two men won't embrace. They won't shake hands.

Standing now in the shack's parlor, John Drew's father lets go of his arm, murmuring, "You're a good fine fellow," and John Drew feels another trill of disgust and walks outdoors.

He discovers the sliver of ice in his own heart. He doesn't care about his brother and sister, he doesn't care for his pathetic father and deadened mother, but if the island girl dies, he'll mourn it for a thousand years.

Spend your time out of doors, he tells himself. Leave that grim invalids' home.

In sullen wanderings, sucking the paws of his gloom, he finds the rowboat buried in the weeds, a blue chipped hull that is beautiful to him.

An old fellow hand-lines catfish and lays trap for otters, and this is his. A bit leaky but it will hold, sure, caulked with pitch, oarlocks strong.

It is time to go. It is time to go. Forget the kite. Make a kite of your own body.

You must fly in the night, when no aged trapper can stop you, when no man swings his angry maul. Take the gunwale in hand and roll it over. You only know this long desire.

The boat slides over the year's last, greasy grass. Shivering water rides up his shins. Much moonlight and seeing is easy.

With an oar's push, the river takes him out into the channel.

He's never used a rowboat—the oars confuse. He seems to move opposite of whatever he desires. He jabs them at the river. Nothing helps.

Speed finds him. Past the reed beds, past the cut. Past the island—he launched too far downriver. Its yellow flag becomes small in the moon. An oar slides up the lock and cracks his eye and makes him recline.

Blood rushes to fill his eye like a bowl. The oar is gone. Spun upriver, he hears a bleating sound like a lamb: the wincing of timbers.

Rocks catch and the hull gives with a sickening crack. Is she on shore waiting for him? No. He knows it now: she has her own frigid, revenging heart.

The boat, small in the moon, lifts and rolls. He's bucked off, and the river takes him, that dark strong indifference that is a drowning river even on the brightest of days, rumbling, dragging—it stings him like a knotted lash.

He sees the lights of heaven, but they are pale and indistinct and more than a little disappointing: Fayetteville, with its new row of gaslights on the river road. He drags himself to the shallows with fistfuls of reeds and spends a long time there, coughing up cold water. John Drew is alive. But he can't go home to face his mother and father, where they mattock small graves from a hillside, and that is a kind of death. He has a sliver of ice. Home is not for him. He lies breathing. He is rushing on.

ROCKING STONE

"SEE HOW IT ROCKS BACK AND forth, sister?"

Uncle Vaughn wasn't a big man, but with little more than a brush of his fingers, the stone fell forward and caught in the crook of rubble beneath. You could push it back from the other side, too, rocking it like a cradle. This boulder—roughly egg-shaped, flecked with green—must have weighed three tons. Uncle Vaughn showed them the magic a few times over.

Neely, one of his two nieces, asked how long it had been that way.

"All my life," said Vaughn. "And some before."

"You're not that old," said G, his other niece.

"I'm a hundred!"

Uncle Vaughn—their great-uncle, really—lived above the garage. He had never married, never left the county but for a spell in the navy, and didn't even own a car, so he was grand company, forever willing to take you berry-picking or deal a hand of rummy for matchsticks. Yet he would twist your ears and hide your toys. There was a touch of madness in that family. Uncle Vaughn once alarmed Neely and G's father by telling him he saw a green sheep climb up over the cliff. A green sheep? their father asked. A green sheep, said Vaughn.

He rocked the stone again. No matter how hard you pushed, it would never crash over the hill in that horrible avalanche that little girls and boys so desire.

They were lucky, said Uncle Vaughn, to have such a wonder on their property. If he had run of things, he would charge people a dollar to see it.

Neely said, "What's in that hole beneath?"

"Maybe it's the Indian treasure." He stooped down and reached into the blackness under the rocking stone, a wonderful place of rattlesnakes and mouse skulls.

G—for Glory, a name she hated—told him to quit that, he'd get pinched under the stone and they'd have to saw off his arm at the joint.

"I'm on a pension," he said—his answer to most demands.

The stone fell forward with a skirling sound.

Vaughn's face went white, drained. "Help!" His body curled with shocking speed, like a muskrat clapped in a snare. "I'm pinched! Oh God!"

Neely began to cry. Uncle Vaughn told them to keep calm, run back to the house, get their mother and a hacksaw. After a while, with the girls too frightened to move, he pulled his arm from the hole and began to giggle.

Neely and G couldn't forgive that. They avoided him for two or three days—no easy task on those small acres—before realizing that without Uncle Vaughn they had little to distract themselves.

When he asked if they wanted to take a walk, they didn't say no.

If the television signal was crackly, Uncle Vaughn was the one who climbed the hill to clear limbs off the line and check the antenna. He brushed aside a fallen grapevine, saying, "You wouldn't think that would foul up the TV, but there you go."

Really, it was too cold this March to wander about, but after a long, drear winter, they couldn't bear being inside. A few bold crocuses offered their buds from the snow. You couldn't smell much of anything in the world. The forest had no life.

Uncle Vaughn asked if they wanted to tilt the rocking stone. Walking there, they saw tree-frog eggs billowing in a swampy place, in horrid, grapelike bunches with black dots in the centers, even though there hadn't been a single warm day.

This time, Uncle Vaughn let the girls rock it back and forth on their own. It took the both of them. Neely and G idly made the stone work its magic. Soon they grew bored. Maybe they could fetch a screwdriver and chisel their names?

Once again, Uncle Vaughn got on his belly. "Let's see if I can fish out Mr. Copperhead."

The girls shot one another a look. They knew what was coming. Uncle Vaughn reached in the hole. "I think there's something in here." Further now, up to his shoulder. Neely rolled her eyes. She gave the stone a big kick. They heard a crack like a tree branch.

"Oh God," Vaughn said. His shoulder was flush to the hole, the arm deep inside.

Neely and G laughed a little. Vaughn's face was turned away from them, probably so they couldn't see him laughing. He didn't move.

"Go get your mother." Then he said nothing more. G climbed off the rock and prodded her uncle. He was unconscious. "Playing possum," she said and gave him a kick. When they heard their father's dairy truck grinding up the road, they went down to see him. After helping unload the galvanized cans, they told of their day with Uncle Vaughn.

Their father pulled Uncle Vaughn out of there, without needing the saw, but the blood on the rock unnerved everyone involved. They were glad when a spring rain washed it away. Uncle Vaughn was never quite the same. He couldn't lift his arm above the shoulder; he went once to church; and when healed up as much as he was going to, he went to the rocking stone with a stick of dynamite. (On hearing of it later, their father said, "A quarter stick would do.") No one was sure where Uncle Vaughn had gotten it. Neely and G wanted to watch, but he wouldn't let them. They had to content themselves with a bang and the thin shower of sand that fell in their hair, all the way over at the house.

Vaughn didn't have much use for children after that.

THE SLOW LEAN OF TIME

T HEY CALLED THE VILLAGE GAULEY BRIDGE after its most discernible feature. In those times, the bridge itself was a swinging affair of rope and boards, enough for one body to cross at a time, and you wouldn't want to in a rattling wind. The river ran thirty feet below. Once, a grand bridge vaulted the Gauley River, before the war, trig enough for horses, wagon trains, even the army that blew it up upon retreat. It was rebuilt, then blasted again to high heaven, this time by the town fathers. They wanted a river clear for logs. So commerce. So the swinging bridge.

For half a morning, Henry Gorby perched on the bridge like a falcon, and small like a falcon. If anyone noticed him up there, he would've been thought eccentric. Most hurried across. The bridge did not inspire confidence. Especially in the men who had roped it. Henry lingered out in the middle in comfort. There was no wind, no one wanting to cross. Despite his slight stature, the rope yawned a bit when he shifted weight. The current bent the weeds below. The Gauley wasn't wide here, but deep, March-green with snowmelt and swollen. Weathered, quartzite ridges loomed on both sides. Henry couldn't see the mountains. He was in the mountains.

Any time a bird or a body flashed through the bankside trees, he was certain it was his cousin Ezekiel coming. Despite the years, he reckoned he'd know Ezekiel: someone brisk and swarthy, from playing out in weather, from a gauge of Lebanese blood. From up here, Henry could see the post office, where they were to meet, and the muddy main drag and every direction going there. Gauley Bridge wasn't much. All paths led to the post office. Ezekiel's letter said two hundred souls lived here. Henry wondered where they all could fit.

Ezekiel wrote yes, he could find a man work.

Below, a wood duck and her raft of young eddied about in worried spirals. It is a duck that lives in the high hollows of trees—Henry didn't know that, he only knew the paving stones of Kanawha City—and he would've been startled at how the ducklings fling themselves from that great height, trusting their downy bodies to God and the soft bounce of a forest floor. Henry, newly seventeen, could paddle and chug along a bit. The ducklings, swimming with prowess, a couple days old, bested him. He could laugh. He had that virtue.

In the Gauley the green fish rose. Henry thought it a piece of bark until it turned in diagonal sweep and showed the grim, pointed mask of its face. It merely drifted to the surface, the length of a child. Then it sank in grassy nothingness with no more motion than a slight, sinuous curve Henry could have imagined. Or was it a lizard? It left like the demon of dreams.

When it returned, Henry was looking in the wrong direction. An awful, heartbroken cackling from the reeds behind. A vortex formed. A hole in the water. Into this, tufts of feathers disappeared. Turning, Henry saw the fish inhale two ducklings. The others broke into the main river and were swept downstream, their mother with them. The thrashing fish tossed water like a canoe blade. Gills flared as it wolfed them down. Henry looked about, frantic, but no one else was there to see, no one to assure him it was true.

Ezekiel never showed. Two shoppers shifted among the rows—the post office was a corner of a store, elbowed in like an afterthought. Henry stood at the stove, which kicked out the heat of a blast furnace. The weather was mild, the brutal fire kept up out of habit. He mooned about and began to sweat. So it took a moment to hear that other voice.

"You looking for Zeke?"

Henry turned to find a clerk. No one called his cousin Zeke. No one he knew.

"Zeke," the clerk said again. "Are you looking for him?"

"I am." Henry moved to the counter.

"Zeke can't make the run. He says go to the staging grounds, it's at Mouth-of-Gauley, that's six mile. Stay on this side of the river and follow the path. Zeke says he's sorry." The clerk added, "Zeke says luck to you."

Henry woke at this jolt. "Wait. What'd you say? He ain't coming?"

"Six miles downriver. You'll see a hoving mountain of logs. The path's muddy but you can make it in three hour. Two if it's dry. It's not." Wearing a clean apron, the clerk stepped out from a half-door and went ferreting in a dark corner. He thunked something heavy on the butcher block. "Zeke says borrow these. He wants them back."

High-topped boots with spikes that bristled from the soles. The leather was gashed and ugly—it had wet and dried a hundred times over—pinched and rucked like a dead face in the desert. But the fresh caulks shined.

"Go on," said the clerk, who had work to do. "They go on your feet."

Henry Gorby lifted a riverman's boots. Had to weigh ten pounds. He felt his heart murmur. The clerk turned away to deal.

Back outside, Henry chucked his own boots away. This was out of character; the Gorbys never tossed shoes, they let them degrade until they slid off midstride. At run's end, flush with money, he would purchase new ones, he would buy many things. Compared to Ezekiel's boots, the scuffed town shoes felt thin as frogskins lashed to your feet. For this sort of life you needed protection.

Mouth-of-Gauley. The Gauley spilled into the Grand River here. Grand? Gauley? South Fork, Back Fork, North Fork of South Branch? A hundred rivers flowed together, joining finally like the veins in an oak leaf, joining in confusion. It took a life to learn them.

Tiered logs, balking above. Tall as hay barns, they humbled the men about them. Henry saw little he recognized. All afternoon that green, awful fish would drift into mind as it had drifted up from the river, as it had killed the ducks.

From the Captain's approach, the men feinted like alley cats. Henry studied him as he paced a furrow into the bank, yelling *shitfire, shitfire, fie*. The Captain would show him how to act, perhaps.

A pike was passed into Henry's hands, and for a moment, he looked maybe as if he knew what he was doing. Henry turned the pike. A fifteen-foot shaft of slender hickory, tipped in an iron barb. Nearby, a smith fashioned more. "Fie! Fie!" The Captain wheeled on the smith, asking why couldn't them goddamned poles be fixed in the last five sodden goddamned days they sit here instead of the very last goddamned minute?

"Five days!" the Captain cried, "and you sit on your pope's nose three"—an untrue thing, for the smith had been working twenty hours straight and was too drowsy to take offense. It was also his burden to pitch-brush the floating arks, the ones docked upriver. Henry didn't know of arks, which that night would haul his sleeping bones.

For a while, Henry hung near the Captain, but not in his line of sight, for the Captain would harry the first thing he saw.

In a lull in the scowling, Henry offered up Ezekiel's letter of recommendation. The Captain took it with a snap. If only Ezekiel were here. Making the long trek from Kanawha City to Gauley Bridge, Henry had been full of hope and vigor in being alone, he didn't mind sleeping out in odd fields or feeling his food bag slacken, because a blood cousin was at the end of this unspooling road. Eighty-five miles to Mouth-of-Gauley if you put string to map, but crooked rivers and ranges made it time-and-again to walk that. Still, Henry made it there on the appointed day. Didn't matter—Ezekiel had run off with a local, to make her his wife. Henry was truly alone, remorseful. He could only hope his obscure bosses would have no use for him, absolve him, turn him home. Let the Captain do it. He would! Look at his face.

The Captain let the precious letter fall in the mud. He looked Henry up and down, saying, "I'd rather have a good big man than a good little man."

Henry didn't know what to say to that. He nodded, and the Captain moved on. Others covered their mouths so not to laugh. Of course there was work waiting for him at Mouth-of-Gauley. There's always work, when you don't want it. Henry could feel the green flimsiness of his bones, their meager reach. He had never stepped upon a stock scale, but if he had, one hundred and five pounds would've been a kind measure. He was fifteen hands high. That, anyone has the tools to gauge. He stood to the withers of few horses. In a great metropolis he could've been a jockey, but was only let to know Kanawha City's sulky draft. His mother took in sewing; his limping father disappeared into the valley's vast salt works daily, except when the war wrecked the works and conscripted their men. Hence the limp and a blue welted hollow in Mr. Gorby's thigh. Mr. Gorby had expected his son to come along, but Henry wanted to see a little world before settling into that, and recalled an aunt complaining endlessly of Ezekiel, who drove logs on the dangerous Grand, all for love of spending money—at run's end, you were paid in full—and they fed and housed you along the way. Aunt Cressy would tell these good things through tears. Henry wasn't allergic to work. He split wood for the Baptist preacher ever since he could lift the maul, and owned hard, small muscles like knots in the cords he split. So Aunt Cressy doomed her sister to share her fate, a wayward Grand River son. Henry wrote Ezekiel care of the Gauley Bridge Post Office. Ezekiel said come on the spring's first run, when logs are without number and the GRC slobbers for drovers.

"Don't take it hard." A fellow stood beside Henry. Awesomely tall, the man wore two pairs of suspenders knotted together. "The Captain's got to insult you three times for every day's pay. That's how he squares outlay to himself. He called me Fatback for years, till I hit him. Tom Sarsen," the giant said, offering a hand.

Henry told him his name.

"Have you drove logs before?" Sarsen pronounced it *druv*.

"No. Not at all. My cousin Ezekiel said he'd get me on."

"Zeke! I know Zeke! Where is he? Where you hiding him? Zeke never run a bank till I showed him how. He didn't know nothing. He's the one I expected more than any."

"I don't know. Supposed to be right here."

"Well, that's a shame. I looked forward to seeing him. Looked forward all winter. I hope he's not sick. Throw yourself in first thing, I say, get your body used to the wet. You and the muskrat. Trying to keep dry is what makes you sick."

They watched the Captain watch a hickory limb. It was screwed down in the river mud and notched at a particular point. When water touched notch, it was time. One hundred and six men, all of them the Captain's, fidgeted on the banks of the Grand. Ten thousand logs, a year's cutting from the headwaters, were stacked above a sloping bank. Touchy drovers stabbed timber with pikes to test the doused-iron heads. Stray slabs of ice came pinwheeling and grinding downriver, the dregs of winter, though it was halfway through March, and green spikes had begun to poke out of the hard, winter-bitten ground. A week before, the river had been frozen solid, then gave up with a pregnant, heaving groan and splintered in a jigsaw puzzle. Now let it clear! Some tipped hats over their eyes, squatted in cold mud, and tried to doze. Others practiced swinging cant hooks, letting them bite peeled logs—red spruce and hickory, white oak and poplar— but not enough to set them tumbling loose. These men the best culled from the timber crews, not afraid to work, or canny enough to slip the Captain a five-dollar bribe. A riverman's pay was double a sawyer's.

Henry didn't know how lucky he was. The Captain felt magnanimous in giving him a chance.

"You hit him?"

"It was wrong of me," Sarsen admitted.

Sarsen admired the Captain, so Henry adjusted his own attitude accordingly. Indeed, Sarsen appreciated the Captain's firm hand. The Captain was like Sarsen's own father, an evangelist. Last season Cap threw a boy off an ark for stealing a shaving kit— threw him off the deck into black nettling waters—and left him there with nothing but the soggy, homespun clothes on his back, which might double as a shroud, who knows?

Sun poured out of a breach in the clouds. The shadow of tiered logs came knifing over the waters. So much timber.

Sarsen whispered, "I'll be captain someday. I been driving for years. I know every shoal. I give them fellers a run for their money." He began to explain, as he would in the coming hours, the Grand's unruly soul, its riprap, its wild currents, its vital mystery. For Sarsen, the world was divided between good, brave drovers and "rat-mouthed fiends." A man named Blind Blake was held out for particular acrimony, called blind because he overlooked the nastiest jams and left them for others, skating away downriver to safety. But most were good and brave, and a gentle, disinterested hand lorded over them all. "I like the Grand River Company. Always treated me square, not like some." Sarsen would've told more, he would've warned Henry against the bad girls of "Rat's Mouth," what he called Mouth-of-Gauley, and not to go abroad of a night into straggling shacks, be glad to leave this palace of temptation behind, but a cry went up.

"Stand back! Stand back!" It was the Captain.

Two drovers shouldered up. They stood at the corners of the first tier and swung cant hooks into the cleats, which, incredibly, held back untold tons of logs. Before Henry could see them pull, a standing wave of timber gave way in an awesome, clattering slouch, the ground rumbled with guttural thumps he felt in his stomach and his vision shook and it all was over. Logs churned the river. Such force would leave his body not big enough to fill a hatbox.

Men slithered out into the water and poled errant logs downstream. The second tier was pulled. The seventh. The tenth. Ten thousand logs and the riverbank a chute of muck.

Saw logs were so dense on the river a duck couldn't light between them. The drovers took up their pikes and tugged on caulked boots that rode up to the calf. Most took penknives and snagged off their trousers at the boot tops, so they wouldn't get sodden and slap-heavy with water. Henry tucked his own into his boots. They had to last him. Men with new footwear punctured the leather to let the water trickle out.

Sarsen told him that was the right way. "You want it to give water like a sieve. Give like a sieve!"

"Mine's fixed already."

"You lied, you said you never run the river! Are you the fugitive living under a name?"

Henry offered up a shy smile at this teasing. His eyes moved subtly, watching Sarsen toss a closed penknife way up into the sun as he spoke. Each time, again, again, Sarsen caught it without looking, effortless calisthenics, like a man with Indian clubs. Always in motion. Never at rest. The knife was so high now, Henry could hardly see.

"These are Ezekiel's," Henry said of his boots. "I got to give them back."

"Oh, I see. Your killer's secret is safe with me," Sarsen said with a lazy wink. He caught the knife and put it away. "How's your pike? You want one so hard and true a cat can't scratch it."

The others broke from Sarsen's path—a sort of deference; they couldn't approach him directly. Everyone was conscious of him. Everyone moved in his orbit. If Sarsen never quit talking, Henry was the only one answering back.

Drovers lined up at a great bear-shaped rock that leapt out into the Grand. The first man climbed up it, looked left, looked right, and stepped off onto a log naked but for the boxed company brand on either end: GRC. Henry shuddered. He expected the man to spin it like a pinwheel and fall into slushy water, but the boots held fast to the peeled, slippery surface. Beaming in his checked shirt, the man used his pike to balance and push off the rock. The log shot forward in the current. He hollered out. A second man eased himself off. In the prickly wind, under a fickle sun that now shined hard, the pair moved nimbly against the silvery rim of river. Henry couldn't see their logs; just two men standing on the waters.

It was his turn to climb. Henry's spiked boots bit the granite with munching sounds. Face hot, legs numb. It didn't seem real. He stood on the crest. It put him in mind of the first time he went bear hunting on Cabin Creek, hounds surging, the black paws slapping them down and cracking skulls, a sense he was in a place he didn't belong.

It was Henry's misfortune to stand out in a crowd, because he wore plain broadcloth, not the fancy shirts of others. "Get up there! Quit acting like cats on a rain barrel! You"—the Captain chopped at Henry—"you was begging me for this job."

Henry stepped off the rock.

The fall seemed a thousand feet. Like a trick, he did not plunge and stop his heart in icy waters, his spiked boots caught, he balanced, he lived. Under his scanty weight, the log dropped an inch. That was all. He let off a whoop.

"Now that sounds right! You was wrong about the boy, Captain! Look at him crook his knees like a veteran!" It was Sarsen shouting down.

Only Sarsen was loved enough to needle without punishment. He did a backflip off the rock, and the log shuddered beneath. Even the grim Captain cheered.

Their lot: to herd stray logs from backwaters; painfully jackbell logs where they beached ashore; and, most important to GRC, break jams that clotted up in rapids. They teased logs out of bankside tangles and had a rough time of it; the willows were hesitant to let anything go.

But Sarsen was strong. He fished a log from behind a boulder where three men couldn't have done the same. In the middle of grueling labor that left most breathless, Sarsen offered up his small sermons: "Note how Marcum takes the inside of a bend? You want to ride that seam. Water's not so fast. Hit that outside bank, you're in a bleeding world of shit, logs'll pile up on you, no place to run. Young bull rides the fast water. Old bull takes it light inside. Right on the edge. He gets old for a reason. Remember how the inside's soft and sweet, like the soft of your trouser pockets." Sarsen's pike flashed deftly in the sun. If his father was an evangelist of the Word, he was an evangelist of water. He had the strength to lift your dead body on a pole and shake you.

Seventeen is a hard year, and there was much to learn. True, Henry Gorby couldn't stretch himself another foot to please a captain, but he could build up muscle and knowledge, he could learn the obscure trade. Sarsen had reached down from the crowd and tapped him for a certain life. Sarsen was the best thing ever to happen to him.

At first the water's rocking made Henry's legs shivery, but soon he guided the sixteen-foot oak like a skiff. He learned the undulation underfoot, its intimations, its English. Henry probed the river; the pike jumped in hand as it caught riverbed, about seven feet under. He watched for deadfalls and the white, killing arms of sycamores that reach low over the waters like women sowing seed. In turn, the Grand offered up its visions: otters that slid down banks like runnels of ink; shoals studded with mussel shells; a tanager stitching itself like Rahab's scarlet thread through crowns of trees; a fox on the bank that seemed to be chuckling. Miles went by. There's no better way to see the country. A snake rode alongside, using his log for shelter. The river broad and smooth. He and others could admire God's handiwork, this place where otters are fish and fish are snakes. The going was easy. But as they went on, manipulation became apparent. GRC had dynamited rapids to make the river nothing but a flume. Every rock scarred with dynamite, entire meanders straightened. Some boulders had iron rings sunk in them like jewelry, where you could lever a ratchet bar and pry a jam open, where you could tether a floating ark. On down, the river was slashed with bone-grinding boulders and ruined dams. Word was the first day wouldn't be too bad a haul of it, until they made Camden-on-Grand, where the river had teeth.

"Tomorrow you'll sweat," he was told, but on that first half day, Henry did little but balance, the arks floating in the distance behind.

The light changed. Night would come on. Henry studied the river. He couldn't tell if it was four foot deep or twenty. The

Grand now seemed cruel and lifeless with snowmelt and mud, but he wasn't afraid.

"Tomorrow we'll break a jam," said Sarsen as he poled along. "Always a jam down there. River pinches in like a girdle. You'll see work." Sarsen smiled. He liked helping these new boys. Charley Parsons, Sull Meeks, Lem Teter, Lem Watson, Zeke, and this one, whatever his name. Like no other, Sarsen could teach a fellow to unlock a jam. The Captain never asked him to; some looked askance at it, but this was the role Sarsen took on. You had to look for key logs, the ones rucked down face-first in the riverbed, even if you couldn't see them, but they were buried there under the mass, it could take all day, it was a matter more for the brain than the eyes. The surface always betrayed you. A hard thing to teach, that. To pick a jam like a lock, to labor in frustration, and then, so startling, it gives way. The crux of the trade. If you could pick, you could always find work. Sarsen had a sense for it. He said key logs held an electric charge and one quivered underwater like a compass needle. Breaking the jam was deadly. The foolish let it bear down in a crush upon them; the wise skated away; and perhaps the wisest never came round at all. Sarsen was wise, he reckoned, and not the wisest. Indeed he thrilled when the jam busted and the jaws began to close—to skate into a side channel at the last second, tasting the electric crackle of death in your mouth—he lived for that moment. In gratitude, Sarsen shared his knowledge freely, learning them the code, but once they learned, the young boys would always forget him, they grew into men, they wouldn't even nod in passing. He could name a dozen right now, on this very river, at this very second. He quit smiling. All his bitterness grew around this black kernel of pain. They wouldn't even look at him. Wouldn't dare shake his hand. They shied like horses.

He called out softly to Henry, who did not answer. This time Sarsen cried with vigor. The boy was looking about, to the reeds, to the shoals, like an idiot.

Henry felt something watching him, some small sort of god.

The fish surfaced in the deep, viridian green. Near five feet long and it sharked beside him with sullen violence. He nearly tumbled. Had it followed him down?

It sank and Sarsen saw it go. He split water, he aimed for a swirl of absence.

"What was it?" Sarsen made a listless figure eight with his pike in the water.

"A big fish. A big long fish." Henry spread his arms to show.

"Musky. They're usual not up this high."

Sarsen was about to say he knew a man who caught one on a yellow plug—but he drove the pike like a piston with both hands.

He lifted the thrashing muskellunge, held it up for the world to see, and let the thrash go out of its body in a final, lurking shudder. He had pierced it through, a third of the way behind its head. Pale out of the water, all dull greenish-bronze and insipid vermiculations, except for reddish fins that reminded Henry of his mother's hard tack candy. It had the teeth of a nasty little dog. Sarsen slid its body down off the shaft, leaving a watery braid of blood. Off the pike, its wound seemed to close. He lifted it by the tail and hollered.

Sarsen could do anything.

The two of them found bunks in a far corner, hunching so not to strike heads on the low ceiling. Others, moving subtle as shadows, gave them a wide berth. The ark smelled of unwashed hair, shaving lotion, moldering clothes. A jungle of socks hung by the stove, from every corner and nail. The river knocked below, snags bumping the hull, scratching, softly thunking. Sarsen's yellow feet dangled over the bunk's edge above.

Henry never had a better night's sleep, and felt fresh when the Captain sent him and Sarsen to a hidden beach that liked to capture logs. There was a bent channel, almost an oxbow, around

Smith's Musselshell Island. Usually four or five men were needed. Maybe the Captain sent the pair alone as a joke, because you had to dig pikes under the beached logs and lever them out, straining your shoulders to the ripping point; perhaps he wanted to set Sarsen down a peg or give little Henry a fright. His aims were mysterious. He dressed no different than any drover, no insignia, not even a watch and chain, but you knew at first glance he was captain.

Sarsen didn't care, he was so primed to break a jam. It had been a long, listless winter. He could jackbell the earth if there was call to. He told Henry, "You got to fetch them out or locals'll steal them. A fellow can get good money on that. Blind Blake hides logs back of there and gets them later. J-grabs, too. He'd steal the eyeballs off your head."

It was good to be alone together. With long, dragging pulls they poled into the still channel, where no current helped them along. A lush place of black cherry and bloomless rhododendron. A thatch of grapevines strained light like a colander.

"What the hell is that?" Something was swimming out to meet them.

"Just mother beaver," Sarsen said.

"No, it ain't."

Then a silver V cutting the current, now the black knot of a dog's head rising. Mystified, Sarsen knelt down on his knees to stroke its floating head. "Hello, little fox!" When the dog tried to put its paws on the log and drag itself up, Sarsen lost balance and slid off in the stinging water. Henry couldn't help himself, letting out a great laugh. Sarsen came up sputtering. After several tries, he crabbed back on the log and shouted the dog off him. It angled away for shore.

Sarsen beat water out of his hat. "Oh shit," he said.

In the shallows, a thin woman pulled up double-fisted piles of duck potatoes. She might as well feed her children air and water.

The woman lifted her head to them, then looked back to the slough. She let out a cry. Sarsen poled on in silence, and Henry followed.

They saw a massive chestnut log, almost four feet across, and two straggling mules hitched to it with a singletree. The log was half ashore, half in water. A black-haired man—a big fellow, who once had meat on his bones but had it no more—was cussing softly but sharply, begging the mules to drag it on. He tugged at their bits, the worst thing he could do. From the slithery drag marks on the ground, it was clear other logs, small ones mules could handle, had been dragged off into the woods.

Henry couldn't help himself. He called out, "What are you doing?"

"We're having a prayer circle," answered the black-haired man.

"Oh shit," Sarsen said again. He cupped his hands and shouted, "Hello! Did you cut them logs?"

Henry shook his head at this piece of nonsense. Even from here he could read GRC stamped on the butt end. A girl, teenage, thin as a mantis, helped the black-haired man with his mules, if you could call holding a tether helping. Three others appeared: two young girls and the woman pulling duck potatoes. She carried them in a wicker trout creel on her hip.

"There's too many people," Sarsen whispered.

The two of them poled closer. Sarsen tapped the chestnut log with his pike. "If this is your property," he said, "then I'm Tom Walker and the devil, too."

"You're no sheriff," said the black-haired man.

"I hope that's true." Sarsen crooned as you would to a touchy horse. "Look here. That belongs to us. Give it here. Look at that mark."

The black-haired man swatted at the nearest mule. His animals couldn't haul it alone. He glanced at his wife and daughters, one of them slack-mouthed and clearly not sound of mind. He seemed to be considering whether to hitch them to the log, too.

"Too much for them," said Sarsen. "You got greedy."

When Henry and Sarsen hopped off onto the shore, the man spoke freely. "This is a deadhead and by rights I can take it."

"It ain't no deadhead. Brand's right there."

The black-haired man bent down to study it.

Sarsen smiled. "See there? Grand River Company."

"You're right." The black-haired man found his toolbox, took out a hatchet, and struck. A crescent of wood flew off. The only thing left was a savaged section of the G. One more blow took care of that. Sarsen did nothing to stop him.

"Now that's river trash for you," Sarsen said. "Henry, that is pure-D river trash."

The black-haired man lifted the hatchet in a half-threatening way. He smiled like one among friends. He had a moustache. "You come take it. You put down that pole and come on over." His voice was stern as a knife, with an edge to it, because he'd shouted himself out on the mules. The family watched this scene with sullen eyes; they had clearly seen others like it. They stood behind in washed-out clothes, the wan color of butternut dye.

Sarsen asked, "What's your name?"

"We seen a hundred thousand trees go this way," said the black-haired man. "I take a couple for my little place up here, won't nobody notice."

"Martin!" his wife hissed.

"Damn it, Mary, let me talk." His voice, once so harsh, grew expansive. "Let me take this, boys. Look around you. All the good chestnut been cut. I can't be going twenty miles up the headwaters to get it, can I? Will it pinch your pocket? No. Let me take this one," he said, on the gentle edge of hysteria. "I'm just splitting fence rails of it."

Sarsen said mildly, "You're going to sell it. You can say if you are."

"No, I'm not. You need good chestnut for good rails."

In the same friendly voice, Sarsen said, "You're going to sell it. Fence rails? Shit. You're too trashy to pen your animals. I can tell by your clothes."

In a dumb, monotonous rhythm, the black-haired man pounded the dull side of the hatchet against his palm. You could see him reckoning what to do. He seemed to appreciate the chance to take a breather. The mules, for their part, couldn't decide whether to sit or stand.

Henry whispered to Sarsen, "This ain't worth fighting over. Really."

"Don't backbite me, son." Sarsen wasn't about to whisper. "Don't get in the road."

"I'm not backbiting. Just, listen. Listen, let's just give it to him. He got a point."

"What? *What?*"

"It's just one."

The black-haired man cried, "See there? That bonny boy says I got a point."

Sarsen took off his wet hat and put it back on. He faced enemies on both sides. He turned to Henry, saying, "Your cousin wouldn't do this way!"

Henry said, "It's one of ten thousand."

Sarsen was aghast at this little child. "If every piece of river trash took one or two, me and you's out of work. All us. This river driving didn't spring up yesterday. This is a damned system!"

"Well, that's true," Henry said. "That's true, too."

"My God, you're overstepping. My God, you was never here till yesterday."

The black-haired man slapped the closest mule with the side of his hatchet. "Get on!" he cried, his voice breaking on a high, merry note. The mule tried to sit. He prodded it again.

"Get on!" Then he buried the hatchet in its shoulder. Blood flew to Sarsen's feet.

"Now damn it," Sarsen shouted, "there's no call for that!"

The man's wife wept in wretched jabs. Sarsen couldn't take it. Swinging his pike, he whacked the cruel fellow across the head. The black-haired man fell, unconscious but not dead. Henry and the eldest girl pulled him from the shallows, so he wouldn't drown in a foot of water. Sarsen began unfastening the chains. Henry tried to help. Sarsen shrugged him off.

Henry asked the woman, "What you want me to do? That animal's in bad shape."

The mule bled in silence, its head lolling about. Somehow it would've been easier to take in if it were howling. The hatchet fell out of its own accord. Yellow adipose tissue shined through, then reddened. The black-haired man kept a neat edge. The blood poured in a curtain with each heart beat. The wound was a rugged flap that peeled from the bone.

"Do you want me to cut its throat?" Henry asked her.

No answer. Henry pulled out his sheath knife—besides Ezekiel's boots, the one thing of value he carried—and killed the animal. It was an act of mercy, but when he finally poled himself away from shore, he would wonder if it would've been more merciful to cut the black-haired man's throat, or the wife's throat, the children's, or his own. When he skated away, he would see the teenage girl watching him. She had violet depths around her eyes. Though he had barely noticed her during the disturbance, Henry fell in love with her. And he would haunt her thoughts. They knew they wouldn't see one another again and were meant to live on in perfect, sentimental balance.

But that was for leaving time. First, he had work to do. Sarsen demanded it. They jammed pikes under the log, levering it out of the mud. It was like tipping a train car onto its side, or trying to. Sarsen could lift his end, but Henry was sweating, moaning, he could feel fiber giving in the pike, he flinched in case it would snap and throw splinters at his eyes. This was the punch of the Captain's possible joke. They needed one more man. Henry added nothing.

Sarsen shouted, "Put your ass into it! Get down low!"

Henry groaned.

All this happening while the woman pitifully made a bandage for her husband's head, gashed between eyebrow and eye.

Sarsen said, "Let it down."

"What?"

"Just leave it go to hell." A dismissive wave of the hand. "You can't do it."

When they poled away from the mud beach, Henry exchanged glances with the girl. His wrists ached, and he tried rolling his shoulders to work out the kink, to show her himself, despite all his failings, all his softheartedness. His sleeve was clammy with the spew of blood.

"I never left a log behind before," said Sarsen.

"I wouldn't worry about it. Captain won't even care—I bet."

"Don't tell him! Don't tell nobody."

Henry said cheerfully, thinking of the girl, "It's funny we never seen that dog again."

Sarsen would not answer.

In silence, they steered around the teardrop island, rejoining the river in its main course. Would the Captain notice they rescued none? No, thank God. In the rally of bodies, the confusion of work, he didn't say a thing. Sarsen exhaled. They rode on, they made the miles. Sarsen left a good space between Henry and himself. As if sweeping aside a curtain, they saw the cutover lands, black acres where the slashings had been burned. There would be a strip of forest again, then cutover, then forest, a brindled senselessness of healthy lands and disaster. At the mouths of feeder streams, silt plumed in the water.

Sarsen finally spoke, but it was to himself. "We got this last year. Look at them big damned stumps."

All had changed. Sarsen had wasted his time on Henry. Henry felt it coming off the man in waves, and he could die of shame. Thoughts of that girl were no comfort.

Here the ruins of a burned gristmill and the new one rising just on down, its great wheel grinding evermore. Here the country baptizing in a chilly, slack hole, the people wading out. Henry thought it a choir singing through open windows until he saw robes billowing in the current. To the staring congregants, he gave a wide berth.

"Them are foot-washers," Sarsen muttered.

Around the bend, drovers shouted. You couldn't make out what they were saying, and then you could.

Jam ahead, they cried. Jam ahead.

This brown, shapeless mass and then, as a tintype picture rises from its cold bath of chemicals, the pieces became distinct, a hillock of buckled logs, some on their sides, some driven in the riverbed, some jutting straight in the air, some planing mysteriously in the current though nothing seemed to hold them back. Henry had dreamed a mountain; this was a sodden carpet. It went on for a hundred yards, and every minute more logs pinned against the mass, increasing its weight, wedging the river shut ever more tightly. Henry's own would soon become part, a thousand held by a single key. Men climbed upon the logs, testing with kicks for loose pieces. A boy with a peavey wrenched at one, shaking his head in disgust.

"This is where you earn your keep! Climb on!" Sarsen was vigorous again, but that was all he said. When Henry most needed counsel, Sarsen would not give.

Like crows on a corpse, men picked at the edges. The Captain shouted, "That's not how you do! You know better than that!" He directed them to the lip of it, the dangerous place. They crawled there out of shame, tried prying a blue channel from the middle. Henry called for random advice. Pull enough mess, it was averred, and the river will do your labor for you.

Grinding wet work. About one of fifty logs Henry prodded at would give way, a little. He teetered on top with water hissing under the logs, though he couldn't see it but for a few black triangles of river. You slipped and scurried, you could fall right through. He looked up at the sound of a dry branch cracking. One fellow had snapped his leg clean. Getting him out of there was a puzzle. Thankfully he fainted away, so they could pass him off like a sack of groceries, that broken leg whanging about. Nauseated, Henry lifted him by the belt. It broke. The boy fell, whacked his leg, cried, and passed out again. The others jeered. Humiliated, Henry lifted the poor boy up in a hug, the broken belt dangling.

Ashore, the Captain fed the boy whiskey and made him a splint and poultice.

While Henry watched this grim medicine, realizing that with a slight injury he could go on home and leave this wet hell forever behind, the logs began to vibrate beneath him. Henry bent down to touch; a vibration ran the maze of his bones. Drovers had picked for hours, opening the slightest channel. Before anyone could shout, the jam gave with a cringe and slung him forward.

Blue and white tumble, a roar of water in his ears. Henry was in the Grand. A boulder loomed, then sucked him under and spat him out the other side. Where was the pike? Foot caught gravel, ankle wrenched. Sarsen ran along the bank. They locked eyes. Sarsen would pluck him out, Sarsen only had to reach down his pike.

All around logs went barreling, any one could crack your skull.

Henry lifted an arm, he waved a hand. Sarsen seemed to hesitate. Henry went under. Sarsen let him go.

They buried him in a talus slide. They had no shovels and were lucky to find him such a place. In this humid country, there are few—bare spots where the mountain shrugs its loose, weathered rock; home to rare, straggling plants; blue rubble; minute, dry prairies. The drovers made a hole in the talus by picking out chunks and scooping up scree with bare hands. Henry didn't look poor in death, only sodden and dusty now, like a confection, with a red smudge on the cord of his neck. They rolled three good boulders on top so animals couldn't dig him up. This was near a place called Gumtree, where locals came with smokers and veils to rob wild hives. In the lore of the river, Henry Gorby is the one who died at Gumtree. He would live on on their tongues, not forever, but a while, the nearest thing to forever.

The Captain asked Sarsen, the evangelist's son, to say a prayer. Sarsen demurred, worn out from lifting boulders, so the Captain said it himself, a mangled psalm.

After, Sarsen slapped a pair of mosquitoes on his rock-dusty hand.

"They'll carry you away drop by drop," the Captain told him.

"Sure enough."

Amazing not more were killed in that tricky spot; more amazing they found Henry's body. Many a Grand River virgin you never saw again. Before lowering Henry in, Sarsen removed his nice boots. No one questioned it, but Sarsen felt the need to explain: he must return them to Zeke, a cousin. Sarsen wasn't specific enough—they wondered if tall Sarsen and scrawny, dark Zeke, always together back then, really were blood?—but they were too exhausted to parse it out. Sarsen was forever wasting his time on one boy or another.

Sarsen finished the run with the heavy pair about his neck, tied at the laces and clanging against him like the strangest jewelry.

On landing at Hinton, where the GRC mill stood, a clerk asked Sarsen with misplaced cheer if the giant worked so hard he needed two pairs to last him through. Sarsen replied only with a glum look. He took his task seriously. Ezekiel would have his boots.

Sarsen later heard there was confusion because someone tried to claim Henry's money at the counter and the rumor was he'd lived, another drowned, with coward Henry sneaking there to draw pay anyhow, perhaps he'd be lost in the crowd. Many believed it.

Sarsen could tell you it wasn't true. He stood in line half-asleep, listening to the bandsaw squeal—it made an awful yowl hitting a knot, you'd think they were sawing up live wildcats in there—and inhaling the vile, gut-shot fumes of the tannery. Branded logs bobbed and thunked in catchment ponds. The gaslights of Hinton pushed against the night. Sarsen was a hundred miles from Gumtree and had labored hard in the weeks since then. The run sped by this year for his liking. He wasn't sure what to do. Go the Elk River run? Little Kanawha? Maybe he could make it in time. He should ask the Captain. Sometimes the Captain went to Greenville, Maine, and perhaps he could use a merry traveling partner. A teetotaler, Sarsen left the others as they went to taverns, brothels, or the infirmary. He had no ear for their biting cant. With pay in hand, he walked to the place where the Grand debauched into the flatness of the Ohio River, a warmish flow where prehistoric fish glided sightlessly in turbid sediments, their open mouths straining unseen sustenance and vile trash—it made no difference to them: the sturgeon with rubbery tails and fecund rituals; gar breaching to fill their grapelike sacs with air; rolling, barrel-chested cats; and monstrous paddlefish with gaping eyes and notochords and boneless drift. The paddlefish wouldn't eat a bait. You could snag them only with treble hooks and lead, or string gill nets bank to bank, which the legislature wanted to outlaw for it fouled up boaters in the night, a harrowing experience. Sarsen had seen the paddlefish, big as rams and just as wild as they thrashed, twisting gill nets, magnificently dying. He once made the mistake of watching what happened next. Some river trash chopped the paddlefish clean in half with a broadax and scooped out bucketfuls of eggs — it made him vomit and the river trash laugh. With glee, they had mended nets. Tonight, the Ohio was one shit-brown swirl. No one fished. He hated ending his run in such a place and was all out of sorts. Hated how the Grand degraded itself by coupling with such an ugly watercourse. Hated how, despite all best efforts, the world will sully you.

No log drives on the Ohio. Long since settled with locks and dams, a storied artery of trade that once split the wilderness in two halves, with its hidebound tales of Blennerhassett and Audubon.

He had Ezekiel's boots in hand. And would return them. But Ezekiel was nowhere to be found.

How could he let Henry drown?

Sarsen was capable, as few are, of great physical courage. He had saved strangers from jams, from rapids, even from a burning ark that sank and snuffed itself hissing in the water. But not for the fool, not for one like fractious little Henry. Sentimental people are the most deadly; Sarsen was one of them. So many of his past charges avoided him; so hard to measure up, so hard not to wither in that annihilating presence.

He wouldn't let himself get sewn up with these children again. He would make the perfect captain.

But there was the matter of Ezekiel, which kept it all in mind. The boots belonged to a man Sarsen admired. A good, brave drover. Ezekiel could work the pike like a lancet; for a while Sarsen called him "The Doctor," but the name never caught.

In the spring of 1876, Sarsen carried them to the staging ground at "Rat's Mouth," but Ezekiel didn't show. Jokes were cracked. Besides that, it was a good run.

1877 the same, boots clopping about Sarsen's bull neck. The year of wicked heat. The boots annoyed the hell out of him. He quenched his own heels in water. From time to time, smiling fire newts drifted to the surface, sipped a bubble of air, and wriggled back down. Like them, he disappeared when winter came, then returned to the river of a spring, back from nowhere, back from nothing. From what he recalled, Ezekiel was like that, too. He lived for the river. Was a mystery.

In 1877, that wicked year, he saw workers grading hills with Fresno plows, and sulky Irish blew a hole in the mountain.

He carried the boots for years, even after the end of the river runs. Despite his knowledge, his candor, his vicious sense of right and wrong, Sarsen would never make captain. The cream, he realized, would not rise. Life awards the middling. The railroads came.

There was no poetry in it. You dragged trees to the grade with horses and, later, steam donkeys and cranes, cradling logs in Alpine cars. Shay engines hauled them away. Workers built corduroy roads and fashioned iron alphabets of grab hooks, each with its own narrow discipline. No need for rivermen, and just a low, gut craving for the river's water, to slake a steam boiler from time to time. You could haul overland, right over the mountain. Now, timbering began in earnest. You could cut away from big rivers, and big rivers were few in the grand scheme of things. In the same grand scheme, Sarsen's river life is a thin, early chapter, more than a footnote, but not the true story. Railroads leveled the forest, fed commerce, changed the place forever. The rivermen had only scratched at it as you would an itch.

All the blasted rivers, all for nothing. On the Grand, the bright scars of dynamite faded. For years, you could buy cheap blasting caps if you knew the place. A sackful made good fishing. Children were shown drill holes in bankside rocks to prove what had happened, and, later, poor sepia pictures of rafts that turned out, on closer inspection, to resemble logs. That and a single iron ring rusting in a midstream boulder. Later still, canoeists would see this oddity and wonder.

Sarsen absorbed all this with wounded grace. He married, and married again. This balm did not soothe. Sarsen's last wife was pretty but almost blind. Her glasses were thick as a turtle's shell and did about as much good. She squinted at him fiercely, no matter how close he stood. They had one child, a boy not bright, but that was fine. He was sweet-tempered, and Sarsen gave him jobs he could undertake with success, let the children all do what they're able to do. It might've softened the father. It did not.

And this business of making a living. Strange. He scrounged. When he had worked the river and didn't give it a passing care, paper bills always found their way into his pocket. Now there was none to be had. He used to say he'd rather be town ratcatcher than a dirty railroad man. When he entered the railroad office, the last to give in, no one could believe it. No one hated the rails more than he.

He'd waited too long. The only work available was building tunnels among Irish. Hot, dusty labor, planting the hard seed of silicosis in your lungs. At a certain hour, lunch was served. Sarsen would lift his plate and walk out to eat alone, so as not to be a railroad man.

All to suture the country with dead rails, which he walked home to Hinton. Sarsen found them hard and punishing to travel upon, by plush car or by your own foot, the steel jolting your joints, "heel-splitters," he called them: you arrived beaten and demoralized at your destination. But water—well, water was pure glide underfoot. Any man could walk on it like Jesus if he had a mind to. Sarsen walked water seven years, then lived twenty-odd of aftermath. When the railroads neared the end of expansion, with a short-line gauge pushed up every hollow, he finished his days pouring shots in a barroom and cleaning glasses with a rag that was eternally damp. He redistributed germs with a democratic flourish. He thought he was doing right—this was the age of miasma theory—and would hate the notion of inflicting sickness. He liked his patrons. He told stories of Grand River days, was thought a raconteur, a living museum.

Sarsen kept the boots behind the bar, to wave about and punctuate a story, but the yeasty room did something to them. When the leather began to green and be unsightly, the owner made him take them home for good.

Sarsen was putting up glasses when Ezekiel walked in.

Walked in, that is, on the arm of his wife.

Sarsen cried, "Zeke! Zeke!"

No answer.

"Do you remember me? Now don't deny me!" Sarsen held a nervous grin. "We fought the river together."

Now, finally, Ezekiel cocked his head, studied the giant in front of him, and offered his tough, little hand. That was all.

It fell to Ezekiel's wife to explain the luckless thing.

Shortly after they had married, Ezekiel took fever, edged up to death with a searing brow, lived, but the fever deafened him. Gradually he lost the power of speech. A passel of faith healers and doctors couldn't slow its decline, no matter the rank, expensive poisons they poured down his throat. He could understand you, but struggled to make his desires known. Or was too proud to. His pride, his wife suspected, was what deadened his tongue.

"He ain't dumb," she said. "People thinks he's dumb. Burns me up. He ain't. He can read your mouth good if you talk *at* him. He's the best leatherworker in Kanawha City. I does the ordering and he works his magic. My book's filled up a year and a half, even if you want a belt. He makes shoes for Senator Gassaway Davis and his pages, too."

Sarsen was slowly realizing this was one of the women of "Rat's Mouth," of the straggling shacks where pay was spent. His charge had not listened.

She didn't want to talk about the river. Sarsen couldn't make up his mind whether to ask Ezekiel or the wife his questions, he kept goggling back and forth. Yes, this was Ezekiel, wizened and gray, but still swarthy, still smiling, his bald pate like a hickory nut. One of the new boys Sarsen taught the trade. Zeke, not twenty years old, "The Doctor," busting jams like human dynamite. He was one you barely had to teach. Just offer encouragement. Sarsen vaguely remembered a night of camaraderie, a stumbling walk back to the arks, arms around shoulders, helping one another onto that bobbing platform that rose and fell, rose and fell, like a carnival game. He had been talked into drinking alcohol. Never again. Or had that happened? Sarsen could not be sure.

Other patrons were getting surly. Sarsen was ignoring them.

"I got something to give you," he told her. "Give him."

Could they meet at their hotel for dinner tomorrow?

They were, she said, on a well-deserved rest. At the New Northern, the finest hotel Sarsen ever set foot in, they were served tiny sandwiches that wouldn't fill you. Sarsen wore his black necktie from work—that much he knew. He was made to check Ezekiel's boots at the cloakroom. That made him nervous, but the attendant looked trustworthy.

To be safe, Sarsen slipped him a coin.

After being poured a coffee in bone-thin china, Sarsen asked about Henry Gorby. Ezekiel didn't even blink, but his wife nodded. "Oh yes. We live next to his people, we thought it best to live near family. They never forgive that boy for running off. They said a Mass for years, there at Our Lady of Lebanon. I'm a convert," she smiled challengingly.

Did they have any idea what happened? No. Sarsen was startled.

Though still teetotal, he told the story with such spirit they thought him a little drunk. Indeed Sarsen was giddy. He explained Henry's goodness, his beatific smile, his feats of strength, how he impressed every drover he met, how he died in the crush. "There at awful Gumtree." By people like Sarsen, the dead are praised all out of sorts at a funeral, and he surely made up for that meager talus prayer.

He ran to the cloakroom, wrenched the boots from the bewildered attendant, and presented them.

"Henry pulled me out the river! He got me out of a spot, he did! When he drowned, I took your boots off him. Here," he said, "by rights they belong to you. He charged me with it. Was the last thing Henry asked me to do."

Henry Gorby had done right: die on the river's crest, at the height of your powers, and the drovers would sing songs about you. Not this long, malingering after. Sarsen would have given his all to trade places. Without shame, he told this to Ezekiel and Ezekiel's wife. He had few memories of a black-haired man and his weeping family; none of Henry's suggestion they betray GRC and give the river trash free rein; none of dead mules and muskellunge thrash; none of letting Henry drown, except the small, niggling realization of something not quite right in the telling. Sarsen's present and his past collided like continental plates, buckling the layers of the old life, making something alarming and new, driving up mountains, faults, declivities. He was a poor geologist. He couldn't map the past. He only wanted to be the Captain.

Ezekiel's wife may have been bothered at being handed moldy leather across white linen, but Ezekiel took the boots with solemnity.

Sarsen feared the wife would ruin the moment, say something chirpy, like, "Them things should be in a museum!" or, "Our leather, sir, is much finer than that!" She did not, only murmuring of Henry Gorby, "What a good boy. I'll tell his mother." Sarsen loved her for it. The whole thing was like a book.

Ezekiel beckoned. He picked up the boots, and Sarsen followed. The wife stayed behind with a coffee and brandy. She warned Ezekiel not to catch cold, as you would a child.

A landing out back of the hotel overlooked the Ohio River in all its cloacal glory. A few tables, scattered chairs, too chilly out for anyone to dine there. Dead leaves pooled in the corners. Ezekiel pulled a small pistol from his jacket. He dropped the boots on a table.

Sarsen flinched. *Oh God, he's going to kill me.*

"It weren't my fault," Sarsen said, raising his hands like a preacher.

Ezekiel swept his arm past him and aimed at the river. He took a potshot at a bobbing bottle in the current. It exploded. Then another. There was a tavern upriver, and drinkers flung their empties over the rail. So this was to be entertainment. Bottles kept coming. Ezekiel liked shooting because he could, ever so slightly, hear the reports, or at least feel them vibrate through his skull, or imagine he could. Since he'd gone deaf, people ascribed to him a vast inner depth and wisdom he did not have. Still flighty old Zeke, not a care in the world. He fished in his pocket for rounds.

Sarsen was rattled on being handed the pistol. He was never much for shooting. His long arm kept the gun sight too far from his eye, just a bitty thing out there you could hardly see, like a comma. He kept apologizing for waste. Ezekiel waved it off, reloading the cylinder for him with petite bullets. After a dozen tries, Sarsen chipped a bottle. It bubbled meekly under. Ezekiel smiled and took back the gun.

Sarsen said, "Your cousin was a good boy. Real good. He was the picture of a good, brave drover. Had a future ahead. He died in them things."

If Ezekiel had any feelings about the long lost cousin, he didn't share. Instead, he squeezed the muscle in Sarsen's arm. It jolted Sarsen. Zeke was forever one of his boys. Ezekiel seemed to be saying, I had some good times in these boots. I earned me some money. I seen some world. I learnt it from you.

In truth, he hardly recalled Sarsen and that life so long ago. Hell, even a cousin met ten times.

"I know," said Sarsen, "exactly how you feel."

So it shook him when Ezekiel tossed the boots over the rail. They bobbed in the current. Ezekiel shot one, then the other. It made Sarsen shiver. The boots would rest among prehistoric fish, fill with mud and tannery sludge, be probed by the mute schools of gar with their speculum bills. Nothing left to touch and consider. Yet they weren't his to keep. He took a bitter pleasure in having done right. He told Ezekiel—looking him full in the face in the nickel wash of moonlight, so his words could be understood—that he should have thrown the boots over himself, years ago. They stood for a heartbeat or two in companionable silence. The boots would drift on. There they were, filling with water.

So the deaf man was startled when Sarsen leapt over the rail after them.

In the darkening night, Ezekiel watched the faint splashing out there in the great wide river. The murky Ohio might take this fool. Then again, he thought, God seems to save those who least merit rescue. He wondered if Sarsen and this blurry cousin had one of those particular friendships you sometimes hear of. What else could explain it? He decided probably not, and reminded himself to buy more shells tomorrow, and laughed at his own lurid, postcard dream.

IN THE SECOND DISTRICT

BLACK SMUDGE ON BOULDERS WIND-SCOURED THE color of bone.

Through riflescopes, the two of us watched the bear cross the saddle. She—a sow black bear for sure—poured her body through the laurel with a loping, liquid gait. Then hounds in chase, driven on lean, pumping haunches. She picked up speed and split through the timberline, where the krummholz lifts in mangled postures. A bear's ungainly way of moving is an illusion. You'd never outrun one. Far behind, hunters dragged themselves up the mountain. They tripped and slid over scree and snow. I counted seven, almost our entire party, a pair of them with an obvious lead. I couldn't tell who they were. Three hundred yards? I'm not good at judging distance. I eased cross-hairs onto the dogs, adjusted the parallax. Shades of hide flickered in and out of focus: Plotts and blueticks, redbones and Treeing Walkers. The sow made the rocky heights, a plateau hovering at four thousand feet.

The rifle was ice against my cheek. In town, the Union Bank clock said twelve degrees. I had no idea how cold it was up here on Dolly Sods. The wind brought tears to my eyes.

A lone birch sapling quivered, a wild clean miss. Someone was shooting. The sow charged through a deadfall. I heard it: limbs snapping against her. And bawling of dogs.

"That's Shovel," my stepbrother said. "He ends on an up note. You hear that?"

He—Conner—wanted a pup out of Shovel's line.

"When will you get one?"

Conner said, "Oh, I don't know. Andy's real jealous of Shovel's pups. Real jealous. Now Shovel come out of Banjo. Now that was a singing dog. That's a redbone."

Even in a moment like this, my stepbrother and I weren't quite sure what to say to one another. We lived in a state of familiar embarrassment.

Another shot. I saw a Plott's stout neck, the head square as a file. Nipping at the bear's ears and ankles, hounds scurried around dolmens of limestone and dipped out of view behind truck-sized boulders. Treble cries clattered on the landscape. Each yelp and bay was distinct. Old men claim the cold does something to it, that singing sounds best come December. The bawling rose in pitch.

We sat in the snowy truck-bed, using the side as a rest. Really, it was the best day Conner and I ever had together, or so it seemed at the time.

Conner tried to hand me a beer, and I said no, thank you. He kept it for himself. It was nine in the morning. The wind had chewed his face red. "Sorry," he said. "I forget." I was probably the only one he knew between eighteen and eighty who didn't drink. People assume you're in AA. I sometimes say I have a stomach condition.

Conner said, "I feel like Patton up here. Or Robert E. You can see it all."

I tuned the scope to 10x. I'd never watched from this angle. We were late for the hunt—Conner put his truck in the ditch on that icy Laneville Road, we had to winch it out—so we drove up Cabin Rock to watch the spectacle unfold. We'd meet up later with the others. The CB crackled in the cab.

The sow forded a run with three great waltz-steps. Hounds swam the chilly water and hit the bank shaking their hides, bodies steaming. I shivered reflexively. Conner laughed at this.

"Rose, you need you a little firewater," he said, draining his beer. (My name is Roosevelt Daugherty.) "Can't hack the cold without it. Makes you feel like a true-blue mountaineer." He struck a heroic pose, the Great Hunter. "We make them northeast libs shiver the night before a presidential election," he said, in a creaky old-timer voice. "Make them shake like a dog shitting razorblades."

I laughed, despite my feelings. He learned that silly voice off my dad. The CB gave out snarls of English, quizzical Chinese, a squall of pink noise. That morning in a strip-mall parking lot, I saw the Chinese merchants from Pittsburgh who huddled around a Chevy Blazer. They sipped tea from Styrofoam cups, listening to a scanner. The bear's gallbladder is said to be an aphrodisiac. They pound the organ into a greasy, yellow concoction and sell it for thousands. Wise fellows, banking on the black market and backward countrymen. Their children graduate Phi Beta Kappa from Princeton and Carnegie Mellon. More power to them.

I said, "I can't see it anymore."

"Me neither. They'll pop back up."

The smell of beer in the cold made me nauseous. I ate a burning handful of snow. This was in my vague year between college and law school. (I had not yet been accepted and was nervous, though everyone else was sure I would turn out okay. Why so sure? I wondered.) Conner was five years younger, but our roles seemed reversed. When I was home on break, he made an effort to take me fishing and hunting. Family was sacred to him.

Like all sentimental people, he would mine that vein till there was nothing left: nothing but bare, scraped rock.

"If you get a shot," he said, "lay down a field of fire. They can take a lot of lead."

I said I would.

"Don't forget," my mother would tell me, "that you are a Methodist."

She repeated this like a koan, to help me through that listless, frustrating year. I worked with my dad and lived with her, an arrangement I definitely preferred. Dad was a small-town lawyer, semisuccessful, and chair of the county Democratic Party, garrulous and hard-drinking and loved by all, a keen mimic, quick with a story. (My mother, chief operating officer at the hospital, is successful without caveat.) I organized for the party in that election year. When I had a free moment, Dad sent me round to the local faithful to gauge their mysterious wants and concerns. I met these sweet old men and women who offered me coffee and pie. In turn, I asked my question. The sweet old woman would say, "I really think the state legislature needs to bring back the death penalty."

That, or reining in the gays, or instituting Castle Doctrine, or plugging the donut hole in Medicare Part D. I loved hearing about that donut.

He sent me to the hard cases, it's true. He acted as if I had forgotten West Virginia. I had gone to Vanderbilt for a year, didn't care for it, and transferred to Middlebury College in Vermont, which I did care for. But I knew our district. I'd grown up hearing it from blowsy pols, union reps, the coal miners, the Democratic Women's luncheon, just as I was forever being handed that same plate of potato salad. They beat it into you at the Jefferson-Jackson Dinner. Dad convinced me to enter law school at the state university, his alma mater, because it would prepare me for life here, for joining his practice. "The Ivy League's a waste," he said. "You can't meet nobody to help you down here, and you'll never come home." But this year was to be my true education: "It's getting hard to hold District Two," he said. "Here's your dance card. Get ready to twist." He lived to set me up for state legislature and then, some distant day, Congress. My grandfather, "The Coal Miner's Friend," represented the Second District for twenty-three years. In his cups, Dad would say, "I could've done it, but these voters won't elect a divorced man. I did what I could for the party, and I think I did it well." No one could argue with that. He died before I could add another disappointment to his disappointed life. After that, the thin tether between my stepbrother and I fell away.

It's so tawdry and plain it hardly merits telling—unless it's your own true life. My parents divorced when I was eleven, and Dad married his secretary as soon as the ink was dry. Yet Mom and Dad took pains to keep a cordial relationship. Even when his drinking and Conner's evils took Dad to his lowest level, Mom would defend him.

The secretary, a brassy country girl from up Birch River, came with a son of her own, Conner. "Instant family, just add water," his law partner fumed. Conner's biological father was a redneck called Shade Tree—as in shade-tree mechanic—and I never knew his real name, Ronzel James Mavety, for ages. Then it clicked. Ronzel, the police-blotter celebrity. Every small place has a family like the Mavetys, known not so much for the ferocity of their crimes but for the regularity of them. They pitch their trash over the hill, jacklight deer, coach their healthy children on how to bilk SSI payments from the government and fool the flintiest social worker. Someone is always pregnant. "Constituents, too," Dad would say. "The lumpenproletariat." So we were as surprised as anyone when Dad rented on Church Street, in full view of everyone we knew, and moved in the secretary and her son. I had trouble imagining what life was like in that alien house. But no one could hold it against Dad forever. Not even my sister, the last holdout. He was the silver-tongued devil, then, and handsome, too.

Conner was silent in class to the point of being thought retarded, but loud and nasty in the hall. I tried to feel for him. I trod the gouged path of my mom's family, ardent Methodists to the marrow: "Your opponent is not your enemy." Mom was sent to England for a conference on the National Health Service—this about the time the Clintons botched their health-care thing—a trip sponsored by the incorporeal think-tank people that essay our politics. When she returned, she taped a picture to our refrigerator, to face me down whenever I craved something cold to fill my belly. It was a snapshot of what she mistook for John Wesley's gravestone, a chiseled memorial in a country churchyard:

LORD LET ME NOT LIVE TO BE USELESS

"Do you hear that Plott?"

"It's deep. Throaty."

"That's right," Conner said. "I could get you one, if you wanted."

I took the scope from my eye. "That would be awesome," I said, and it would be. I loved the dogs—Conner felt obvious glee in how closely I listened to them sing. We liked Shovel best, a redbone named for his triangular head. He tracked by scent, huge ears flapping in the wind, driving air and stench to his nose like a set of bellows. So did the German Plotts. The others were strictly sight-hunters with jaws like vises; once such see a bear they don't let up until they die or are wrenched off. Their bravery gives you the luxury of distance, of safety. Unless you chase a bear into the rocks. You want a bear to tree, not cave. That's when accidents happen.

The sow doubled back. She couldn't outrun them. She dropped her shoulder and struck a bluetick. It rolled twice and gathered itself up. The pair of hunters in the lead picked over the boulders, trying to make firing range, orange jackets as bright as fires against the rock.

"See them teeth flashing?"

"The dog or the bear?"

"Hell, the both of them," Conner said with a grin. "You having a good time?"

"I'm having a great time."

He asked me his question in such a plaintive voice—you couldn't help but feel a stab of love, remembering he was seventeen. He knew nothing of the world outside the county. It made me feel awful—a knife in my guts—for the embarrassment I felt for Dad's second family.

You're not supposed to glass people through a riflescope, but our guns were unloaded. The two hunters turned out to be a young boy and a red-bearded, fat fellow.

"It's Bud and Andy."

I didn't know them. The boy lifted the rifle to his shoulder and fired. Conner cheered, "Good work, Bud!"

The wide black rump came wallowing out of the brambles. The sow dragged a hind leg. The bullet had licked her. She dove into a shallow cave. Dogs boiled at the mouth. A paw reached from a crevice and swatted one down. Bud and Andy stood less than fifty yards from the cave. They angled for that snappish ball of animals.

"Oh man, Bud's in for it. He never done this before. I hope Buddy took him a good dump this morning, else he'll shit himself for sure. See its head pop out? You see?"

I did. "They're going into the cave," I said.

"Wow."

A hesitation, a stutter. The boy didn't move. Another hound was slapped, hard. Shovel, the redbone. My stomach roiled.

I could see the man, this Andy, gesturing with a shiny pistol. The hounds spun in tight circles, tilting their wattled throats to heaven. I imagined one torn apart, its body broken like a cigar. They are killed sometimes. Skulls bitten. Rib cages winking out.

The boy wouldn't go in after the crippled bear.

Conner said, "My God, what a pussy. I heard him talking big the other night. I'm going to rag him. Aw, Bud! He won't live it down. That's for sure."

Why not let it go? This was the brutal affect he shared with my dad. Both could say things that stunned me, that made me feel slow. When I'd told Dad I was going bear hunting, which I once heard him call "the white trash Olympics," he said, "You need to mix with people like that. Someday you'll have redneck friends to vouch for you. Makes a good ad."

My left eye began to twitch. On the mountainside, Andy pushed the boy out of the way with a big, square hand. The rocks swallowed up his blazing jacket.

Conner said, "Gun in one hand, flashlight in the other. I been there a few times myself. You should smell it in there. A bear is rank. I about pissed myself the first time. I'm lying. I did!" Conner leaned back and sipped another beer. "You only get so many shots in your life. Especially your first. Took me four years. I've got two bears, almost three. I'm pretty lucky. You'll get yours someday, Rose. Buddy fucked himself over. It's one thing to get fucked by somebody else!"

"How old is he?"

"Bud? Oh, I don't know. Thirteen, fourteen. Guess his balls ain't dropped."

We heard Andy drain the clip. *Popopopopopopopop. Pop.*

Pop. The cave muffled the sounds and amplified them at the same time—it's hard to describe. You have to hear it for yourself.

We waited. We waited. Even the dogs hushed. Andy didn't come out.

Conner slapped my arm. "Something's wrong. Something's wrong." We ran to find them, sliding down the mountain, down to whatever horror below.

Living with someone like Conner: You arrive slowly at your destination, where you have a life and he's in the penitentiary, completely estranged, having given out suffering to everyone he knows and many strangers besides, but in the meantime you must live through the agony, pretending this time, this time, he'll set himself right. ("Destination": I despise Calvinism and it reduces me to use the word. Conner made choices. I tell myself this. I tell the world this.) For Dad, it felt like being skinned. Soon, even magistrate friends and a helpful sheriff couldn't slow it down. He loved Conner in a way he couldn't love me; Conner needed saving. Those last three years, Dad was bloated and puffy, "from the medication," he said, but you could see the red-rimmed eyes sloshing around his head. He shuttered his office.

Sometimes I tell my wife, "It's not right that I look down on them."

This after I wire a couple thousand dollars without telling her. Purely out of shame, at the pride I feel in not sharing a drop of blood. Conner needs to make bail. He is surely guilty. We don't have that money to spare. She is heavily pregnant, her belly bowed out, the prow of a ship. I tell myself this is the last time.

She says, "They should be looked down upon. That's what scares you."

When these feelings well inside me, I drive up Dolly Sods. Come a winter I put chains on the tires to handle that wicked Laneville Road.

Dolly Sods is a lost tundra, a sliver of Canada sixteen hundred miles below where it ought to be, left there when the glaciers took their tall walk north, scrawling rivers on the land. Windswept boulderfields and twisted aspen, tannic rivers and sphagnum bogs, reindeer moss and snowshoe hares. Spruce trees gnarled and flagged by the winds. Carnivorous flora: pitcher plants and sundews, uncanny and Pliocene. Flies slip down gullets, or feel the snap-embrace of sticky tentacles. In summer, it's all flaming azaleas and larkspur, but winter turns it cold and hard as a forged blade. In the distant past, a German and his Huguenot wife tried eking out a thin sustenance on the plateau, clearing a few slashes of pasture—sods—for sheep and cattle. Nine feet of snow fell that winter, foundered the herds, and drove them back to the valley, but the name persists. Since we can't read, write, or talk, Johann Dahle's pasture became Dolly Sods. No one lives here. It's so desolate that the army practiced artillery here for the European Theater. Hikers find live shells that rust in the rocks. The army returned in the Clinton years and detonated fifteen. When I was young, we climbed up here to gather huckleberries and watch from arm's length as strange birds bathed themselves like mice in the dust of boulders. My grandfather lifted one blinking in the cup of his palm. Did that really happen? It's what I remember. We hiked to the Roaring Plains. Wind snapped our clothes. Sun and clouds, raptors kiting in the thermals as if tethered with wire. We watched eagles a thousand feet below. My grandfather took my little hand in his. He pointed out the features: the Canaan Valley, the Blackwater River, the shuttered Poor Farm, the grade school named for him, the strip mines, the quarry, the Coastal Timber yard, Highway 33, Moatstown with its dwindling black community, Circleville née Zirkelville, Snowy Mountain, Mare Camp Knob, the fields chalked with grazing sheep, the Daugherty Home—ours—and so much else. "It gave me the grandest pleasure to serve the people of these counties. In times of fear and uncertainty, this place sustained me. In the Philippines or Washington or anywhere." It's the only memory I have of him.

Andy—Andy Mavety, I suppose—staggered from the cave on his son's shoulder. His voice slurred a little, he seemed almost drunk, hopping on one leg. Thin lines of blood trickled from the corners of his mouth, as if he'd tried to swallow a spoonful of paint. He dabbed at his lips. With the full authority of my Eagle Scout first aid, I made him sit on a flat rock and open his mouth. He had bitten deep the tip of his tongue.

Andy was trying not to cry. His face was red as his beard. Gingerly, Conner unlaced Andy's boot and slipped it off him.

His son should have done that, I thought. Bud stood there, abashed, rifle slung.

The foot flopped about in a way it shouldn't. The ankle was broken—you imagined you could hear the bones scraping together. Andy was a tough old bird. No, he said, no ambulance. They'd never make it up here, and even if they did, he didn't want to pay the bill. "Somebody just drive me after we skin it out, is all I ask." Beads of sweat formed on his forehead and face. He seemed to flutter in and out, like to fall off the rock. "I hate sitting in that fucking emergency room. Keep you for hours."

The hunters winced at the sight of it. Already beginning to darken, the ankle would be ratsnake-black within the hour. Conner moved it. Andy sucked in a sharp breath. He'd slipped and fallen as the dogs swarmed about in the cave, gun kicking in the darkness. "Couldn't see the fucker," Andy said. "Should've took a flashlight."

"You didn't have a light?"

"Stupid of me. I forgot. Too old for that kind of shit. Young man's game."

I asked, "How's it feel?"

Conner snorted. "Shitty, I bet."

Andy began to protest he was just fine. He looked over at his sheepish son. "Twisted, is all. I'll be running laps tomorrow." He smiled for Bud's benefit. Bud wouldn't meet his gaze.

Someone I didn't know, a man about thirty, stripped off his jacket and flannel and gave me the t-shirt beneath. The man's torso was awfully pale, and tattoos shined bluely from his skin. All the fellows looked to be state-pen alumni—oxycodone people. I cut the shirt and made a wrap, as you would for a sprain. Now I know that was the wrong thing to do. All I did was ratchet up the pain.

Andy was given a couple fat white pills to get him through.

The dog you couldn't do much for. Shovel's ear was torn almost in two, ghastly, flapping like a piece of lunch meat. I tried scratching Shovel's bony skull to calm him, but even then, he was proud and aloof, like the cotton-field debs I met at Vanderbilt.

Conner took Shovel's head roughly in hand. The dog yelped and bled in earnest now. He frowned at the claw-tattered ear. Someone produced a medical kit, no bigger than a flask. Conner asked me to hold the dog, which whined and shivered in my arms. Conner stitched the ear together the best he could with a steel needle and gut. It wasn't Conner's dog, but he liked doctoring, perhaps because he'd failed biology three semesters in a row. Dad had to browbeat him to stay in school. The fights were epic howlers. You'd think he was sending the kid to Bergen-Belsen.

Conner looked at me. Gruffly, he said, "You look like you got something to say."

He meant, as he always did, You're not any better than me.

"Not really," I said.

"There's amoxicillin in the box."

He forced a pill down the dog, clamping its mouth, massaging its throat. Shovel walked away on unsteady legs. The doctoring didn't look sound, but I held my tongue.

We young fellows went into the cave. Bud fell in to help. Neither Conner nor I mentioned what he'd done, the way he refused to go inside and kill the bear. If not for me, the others might never have found out at all.

The cave smelled of grease and afterbirth, though she seemed to be a barren sow. The flashlight beam picked up a glint of light like a scrap of aluminum foil. I scooped up Andy's pistol—an off-brand .40 S&W—out of the mud and stuck it in my pocket. The smell shifted to rancid milk: the gut-shot bear. In those confines, it was enough to make you ill.

A backbreaker dragging her out. We propped her on rocks, blood dripping from the muzzle. The dogs milled obsessively about her. She stood five-ten, my height, and maybe two hundred pounds before dressing: very good for West Virginia. It would've been a fine first bear for Bud. For anyone. I felt a twinge of jealousy. I worked out the claws and whistled. I wished it were mine. Conner opened the jaws wide and stuck his neck in between, feeling the yellow fangs on his neck. Everyone laughed.

"Christ," Conner said, pulling out and letting the mouth snap shut. "Teeth stinks."

A fellow said to Bud, "Hell of a bear. You ought to be proud."

Bud stood there, frozen, unanswering, just a bashful, quivering smile.

Andy said, "You done good, pal. You can brag on that one."

Andy was telling us that Bud had killed it! He didn't know Conner and I had seen it all. Conner looked at me, muttering something obscene.

The lie made me unspeakably angry. I hated that lying child.

The shirtless, jailbird-looking guy (who had since pulled on an open jacket that read NOTHING FINER THAN A PIPELINER in stylized letters) took out a cell phone and snapped a picture of the bear. I remember that because no one here had cell phones in those years; the county didn't even have a tower. Never would, until the ski resort demanded one. That was the first phone I encountered that could take pictures. Prideful, he showed us how it worked.

There were no normal trees, nothing with which to carry out the bear. Instead, we made a harness of rope and skidded it into a draw with road access. The exertion cut the cold. Andy hobbled behind, wincing, leaning on Bud. We hoisted the bear over the embankment with one final groan and onto the road. Eyes gone blue. Body stiffening. The hounds followed, leaping to lick blood from the coat. Conner socked them back with the ball of a fist.

When I looked at Bud, the inexplicable anger returned. The cold poison flooded me—the cold poison that is my life.

Thirty minutes later, we had a circle of trucks. We fixed a log-chain around the bear's neck and made a gallows from a stout limb. As I cranked the winch, the chain yawned and tightened as it drew out the slack. The bear levitated as if wanting to stand again. Someone backed Andy's truck under so we could stand in the bed and gut her deftly. The innards fell with slapping sounds on a garbage bag and steamed.

Crawling uphill in the Blazer, the Chinese came, and we got ready to split the bear: head and hide to the one who killed it, the meat divided equally among us, the gallbladder to the lead-dog's owner, to defray the possible cost of death. Casting glances for game wardens, the Chinese weighed the gallbladder with scales and paid Andy a thin stack of fifty-dollar bills. The last warden used to take a little taste, but he had retired and times had changed. They slid the gallbladder into a Mason jar. It was a greenish-black sac, heavy with bile and big enough to fill my palm. Frowning, Andy held up the money.

This female bear, said the Chinese, isn't as valuable. Andy said they were fucking liars. They'll say it's male anyhow. With a smile, he demanded full market value.

The bartering seemed to soothe his pain, but really, the synthetic morphine was in his bloodstream now.

A middle-aged Chinese man in a really nice Filson jacket approached me. He was handsome and dignified, the color of magnolias, and had no accent. In fact, he sounded more American than any of us locals, us who had no ties to any other land, with our twang that people at college—even my professors—made fun of behind my back, even when I took pains to lessen it.

The well-spoken Chinese said, "This is a fine bear, truly." Her body swayed and drooled redly in the snow. "Particularly for a female."

For some reason, I felt an urge to talk with him, which I always do with foreigners here, to show them we are good people. "She run the dogs hard," I said, "this one especially."

Then I realized two things: that I was just more white trash to him, and that he was a hired interpreter for the other Chinese.

"My name is Jimmy Carter," he said. "It is a pleasure meeting you."

"Holy shit!" Conner cried out, slapping his knee. "We got us a commander in chief."

"You were ahead of your time," I told the man. "America wasn't ready for you. They weren't right to make fun of your malaise." In the waiting room of Dad's practice, there was a handshake picture signed to Carter's "friend in the mountains," George Daugherty, "with the greatest of thanks."

I expected the Chinese man, this Jimmy Carter, to laugh, but he didn't respond at all. He seemed to have no idea of the displaced magic of his name. Grinning in a blank way that rattled me. Maybe the man was stolid, or had picked the name out of the Yellow Pages. Conner's face said, Get a load of this crazy-ass chink. The other Chinese stood listening in the snow. Shovel wormed his head into my lap.

Finally I asked him, "Are you doing good business?"

"Oh yes. A great season in the Smokehole Canyon."

"We heard on the radio."

"Yes, four hundred pounds. A monster! John McCrory there told me a joke. He said, 'What do you call a farmer who raises goats *and* sheep?'"

"What?"

"A bisexual."

We laughed. I said, "I thought you were going to say, 'A bigamist.'"

Jimmy Carter let out a great air-rattling belly laugh. "Oh my," he said, wiping tears with the heel of his hand. "That's good. Like a Mormon. Who killed this bear?"

I would reveal the boy's lie. Or make his father deny it. Shovel began to tense and whimper in my arms. I nodded my head at Andy, about twenty feet away. "Guy over there on the tailgate," I said to Jimmy Carter. "The fat one in the orange. He went into a cave after it."

Andy could hear. He shot me a frightened look. He knew.

"You don't say?" Jimmy Carter asked. "Which one? I want to congratulate him."

I've thought of this moment lately, of what I should have said—or more appropriately, not said. At the time, I couldn't have known I would drop out of law school, answer the call, go to seminary. My church is in walking distance of the building in which I once read law before throwing it over. When I made a name for myself, the conference gave me a large church, passing over older clergy, for which I'm not loved. Now I'm caught in the same snarls I would have been had I become a politician: Dad's revenge. I didn't know it until my trip to Dallas. I went there to argue with the troglodytes, southern bishops who would defrock us. The issue was homosexuality; some of us had presided over such marriage ceremonies, against official policy, admittedly making a spectacle of ourselves. I hadn't done so myself—not brave enough—but I was there to advocate for those who had. I stayed in a brightly lit hotel. I told the kindly people of Texas, No, I have not yet seen the grassy knoll. Across the table, these men hated me. Useless. Dad would have charmed them, accomplished something. My failure is punishment come down upon me.

"Guy with the red beard," I said, gesturing. "He killed it."

Andy sat back on the tailgate. The blush returned to his face. He looked at me. He looked at Conner. Jimmy Carter made a beeline for him.

Turning to me, Conner gave out a clipped, mirthless laugh. "This'll do," he said. "This'll do." I saw the flashing in his eyes. He approved.

Andy was saying miserably, "No, no, my son got it."

"Oh, my apologies. They say you shot it."

"Well." Andy looked at his ankle as if it would speak. "I don't know."

"My apologies." Turning now to Bud, Jimmy Carter said, "Congratulations on your first bear. This one is truly impressive. It is a great beginning. Second-nicest we've seen today."

Bud mumbled his thanks.

"You went into that cave?" Jimmy Carter asked. "You bear hunters are crazy. You could have been killed! Tell the story. Go ahead."

When Bud didn't respond, Jimmy Carter thought he'd insulted the boy. He backed up, gesticulating. "No, I do not mean to say you are stupid or anything, necessarily. I am floored by your bravery. I could never do a thing like that. Truly. I am."

Tossing a beer can in the snow, Andy spoke up. His face was pinched. He gave his son a look that could chisel granite.

"Yeah, that's right. By God, he risked his ass."

The other hunters passed one another glances. Miners, mechanics, outlaws. They were realizing the truth of the matter: a whisper in the blood told them so. They could break down engines, run bulldozers, live with comfort in their own skin. I wasn't one of them, with their easy aggression, their jokes, their settling of scores. It's no wonder I prefer the company of women. The dam of ice had breached inside. Immediately I felt regret.

My stepbrother called out, "You done a good job, Buddy!"

Shoulders hunched, the boy crammed himself into his person. Dissolving.

Jimmy Carter saved the day, asking mildly, "Do you plan on hunting tomorrow?"

"Not now," Andy said, then cussed his ankle and his luck. "I got work tomorrow. Boss is gonna flip. Don't even want to think about it. These boys will all be out."

"Yeah, I got to get me a bear this season," Conner said. "Heading overseas and all. I'm going into the Marines."

This was news to me.

Jimmy Carter wished him the best of luck. "Speaking as one who chose his citizenship, I can say I appreciate your service more than most."

The first flag-waving year of that televised war, before it soured, when the scene was grim for our party. Dad sulked. "Start a war, win elections. Might as well not field a candidate. Just take our ball and go home." Several months after the hunt, when Conner was still skulking around the county, I asked my dad about it. Dad said, "My God, how your brother lies. Can you imagine him listening to a superior? He's a little chickenshit chickenhawk. I finally drove him to the recruiter. He wouldn't get out of the car."

Conner shook Jimmy Carter's hand and said he appreciated the hell out of it. "I need to do me some fucking before I go. Patriotic, are you? Got any daughters?"

Jimmy Carter laughed again. "Only sons."

"Are they pretty?"

Andy hooted. "I'd give a arm and a leg to be that age again. I'd hop after them on the bloody stumps."

After bidding the Chinese goodbye, we skinned the bear down to red flesh and white sinew, soon to be rendered into hams. A naked bear is too human for words. We lifted yellow blankets of fat and piled them, where the hounds rolled and gobbled and burrowed in the mounds. Bud threw in and worked hard, trying to make up for being himself.

I hated to pull my red arms from the carcass, because it warmed them so. Soon we'd saw off the head, and the sow's body would drop into the bed with an axle-shaking thump.

"Sorry you didn't get yours," Conner told me after. "Keep the faith. You'll get him. This storm coming, we'll call it a day. Andy like that, too." Soon he'd fly across the waters and become a russet smudge on the sands, his face a void. Eyes, gone. Jaw, gone—at least, that's what I pictured at the time, before I knew it was just another lie. I wanted to tell him not to go. Maybe he should have gone. Get him away from this tar pit of a place. Could the military have fixed him? Yet I preach that war is unspeakably wrong. He grabbed up the leg of a yelping bluetick and examined the paw. "Cut all to hell. This hard crusty snow is like knives on their pads." The dog licked its feet, which had turned the snow to a pink slush, as if we'd broken a watermelon for lunch.

I checked Shovel's stitches and noticed him bleeding a bit about the ears, but then he ran off to slurp some snow. I was ready to go home. Someone shot a whiskey bottle sitting in the ditch. It disappeared in a cloud of glass and a cheer went up.

When it happened, we were discussing who'd take home the tenderloin, the finest meat. You take it. No, you. Shovel whimpered at my boots, fell, and began to seize.

I clamped my hands on the dog's head and called out. Warm blood trickled over the webs of my fingers. I used my thumbs to parse the skin. Shovel shrieked in a way you don't expect from a dog. He bled from the mouth and the nose. A swollen brain, something ripped and bleeding beneath the skull, where the bear's teeth had punched through. Shovel bucked, eyes rolling. Something so disturbing about the sick-animal thrash against my arms.

Andy hollered, "Where's my gun?"

It took me a second. I took out the pistol and handed it over. I had forgotten I had it.

With the heel of his hand, Andy slid in a fresh magazine with an oily click. He staggered off the tailgate, moving somehow on that broken peg of a foot, and held the pistol out to Bud.

"Your bear," he said. "Your job."

Bud didn't move.

"Come on," Andy said, seething now. "Time you done some growing up."

Bud's voice wasn't as steady as it should have been. "I'll take him to the vet. I'll pay for it, I'll use my own money."

The men jeered, spitting on the snow, telling him to suck it up. I watched the kid choke something back, swallowing it slowly, barely, like a peach pit.

He took the pistol and held it, doing nothing.

Shovel whined in an awful, wounded way, like we were cutting his tail off.

Conner shouldered up. "Do it, damn it. He's in pain."

I turned away. I didn't want to see Shovel's face break open. A moment later, I heard the distinct crack of a dry-fire. I turned and looked.

Conner said, "You got to put a bullet in the chamber, genius! You little liar. Give me that shitty fake Glock." He jerked the live pistol from the boy's hand. He pulled up a round and swung on Shovel's brain.

I had forgotten to check the barrel for mud and snow.

A metallic belch and the pistol split its length in a flash of fire. Conner dropped to his knees. Everyone shouting. The dogs were silent. I remember how chilling that was. I was afraid to look.

The gun had exploded in his hand. Conner unclenched his fingers. He gazed at his hand in wonder. There was no flurry of blood and bone, only the gun barrel in many slivers upon the snow. It should have taken off his arm. He was lucky then. He looked again and again, for the slightest nick, the slightest flaw. You could have done it a thousand times over, and it wouldn't have happened this way.

It took me a while to register the dog was dead at our feet. No one would touch it.

There is a little white house outside of town. It stands away from the road. All alone. You can just see the driveway and a red hint of door through the laurel.

There is no death penalty in this state, but if there were, Conner and his friend, the one who stripped off his shirt that day, surely would have gotten it. They emptied her medicine cabinet for pills. They took less than fifty dollars from her purse. It was night. They beat her to death with their hands. Eighty years old. They beat her with a savagery no one could understand. Why did he kill her? He didn't have to. In a just world, lightning or flood would level that place. I drive by it again and again.

This is one of many houses.

Her name was Angela Sayles. One of those old sweet women I visited on my rounds. She had, I remember, skin so white and clear, like cigarette paper. You could see the bones fluttering in her hands. She had freckles across the bridge of her nose and a pleasing loud laugh you couldn't imagine from her slight body.

ACKNOWLEDGMENTS

"Something You Can't Live Without" first appeared in *Oxford American* (Spring 2010) and was anthologized in *PEN/O. Henry Prize Stories 2011: The Best Stories of the Year.* "Mates" appeared in *the minnesota review* (Fall 2014). "Natural Resources" appeared in *Baltimore Review* (Spring 2013). "Gauley Season" appeared in *West Branch* (Summer/Fall 2013) and was anthologized in *Best American Mystery Stories 2014.* "Telemetry" appeared in *Ploughshares* (Winter 2012-2013). "The Island in the Gorge of the Great River" appeared in *Ecotone* (Spring 2014). "Rocking Stone" appeared on the *Tin House* website (May 31, 2013). "The Slow Lean of Time" appeared in *American Short Fiction* (Spring 2014). "In the Second District" appeared as "Destinations" in *Mississippi Review* (Winter 2013-2014).

The author wishes to thank the editors and magazines that first published these stories, as well as the following institutions and people who helped make this book possible: the University of Iowa, the Fine Arts Work Center, the Michener-Copernicus Society of America, the Jentel Foundation, the St. Botolph Club Foundation, Key West Literary Seminars, Sarabande Books, Sarah Gorham, Kristen Radtke, Ariel Lewiton, Lydia Millet, Janet Silver, Charles D'Ambrosio, Allan Gurganus, Lan Samantha Chang, Connie Brothers, Deb West, Jan Zenisek, Roger Skillings, Salvatore Scibona, Jaimy Gordon, James Alan McPherson, and Arlo Haskell.

ABOUT THE AUTHOR

MATTHEW NEILL NULL is the author of the novel *Honey from the Lion* (Lookout Books). A graduate of the Iowa Writers' Workshop and a winner of the PEN/O. Henry Award, his short fiction has appeared in *Oxford American, Ploughshares, Mississippi Review, American Short Fiction, Best American Mystery Stories, Ecotone,* and elsewhere. He divides his time between West Virginia and Provincetown, Massachusetts, where he coordinates the writing fellowship at the Fine Arts Work Center.

Sarabande Books is a nonprofit literary press located in Louisville, KY, and Brooklyn, NY. Founded in 1994 to champion poetry, short fiction, and essay, we are committed to creating lasting editions that honor exceptional writing. For more information, please visit sarabandebooks.org.